Faith
Countryman

ALSO BY LORI HARTMAN GERVASI

Nonfiction

Fight Like a Girl . . . and Win: Defense Decisions for Women

Faith Countryman

A NOVEL

LORI HARTMAN GERVASI

Waterfall
PRESS

Text copyright © 2016 by Lori Hartman Gervasi
All rights reserved.

Scripture quotations marked (NIV) are taken from the Holy Bible, New International Version, NIV. Copyright © 1973, 1978, 1984, 2011 by Biblica, Inc. Used by permission of Zondervan. All rights reserved worldwide. www.zondervan.com The "NIV" and "New International Version" are trademarks registered in the United States Patent and Trademark Office by Biblica, Inc.

Published by Waterfall Press, Grand Haven, Michigan

www.brilliancepublishing.com

Amazon, the Amazon logo, and Waterfall Press are trademarks of Amazon.com, Inc., or its affiliates.

ISBN-13: 9781503936294
ISBN-10: 1503936295

Cover design by Shasti O'Leary Soudant

Printed in the United States of America

For Frank
and
Tyler and Luke

"Now to each one the manifestation of the Spirit is given for the common good. To one there is given through the Spirit a message of wisdom, to another a message of knowledge by means of the same Spirit, to another faith by the same Spirit, to another gifts of healing by that one Spirit, to another miraculous powers, to another prophecy, to another distinguishing between spirits, to another speaking in different kinds of tongues, and to still another the interpretation of tongues. All these are the work of one and the same Spirit, and he distributes them to each one, just as he determines."

1 Corinthians 12:7–11 (NIV)

"Dear friend, I pray that you may enjoy good health and that all may go well with you, even as your soul is getting along well."

3 John 2 (NIV)

MODESTO,
CALIFORNIA

~

C hances were slim that I was conceived from anything more than a wisp of Saturday night desire, conjured up after pie and coffee on the porch swing, and threaded along by a good shake of contrived longing. But when I was born to this world, it was with roused intention. Headfirst. Eyes open. In the middle of a violent rainstorm. Weather that proved so devastating, it nearly ruined the life of every farmer in our county.

When that water broke loose from the sky, it came at us like the dam caved in. Described for years by folks in Modesto as of biblical proportions, the storm left us sopping wet for weeks, yet reeling from the effects much longer. A decade later, it was still the big excuse for anything that happened to go wrong. You name it—broken marriages, miscarriages, deaths, acts of infidelity, and every sickness under the sun. Even blamed for a pack of mangy-bald, rawboned tomcats running loose downtown.

"If only it hadn't poured so much," the neighbors whined. Or "Too bad we lost everything that year."

For seven days straight, we took our licks. Shops and schools closed. Power lines snapped and whipped about. Crops submerged in sludge, as skunks and possum drowned, and baby calves floated in their own pooling pastures.

All the while, our big two-story in the outskirts off Rumble Road was drenched clear through. With no power for hours at a time, the entire structure rode out much of the storm by candlelight, with massive creaks and groans as wind shook windowpanes to wood frames while water crash-landed against the roof.

"I had no idea this was coming at your time, Eva," Daddy told Mama, frowning at the dark skies.

No one expected it. This arctic front that suddenly veered off course, swirling south and somersaulting inland. When it surged over the Central Valley, our farmers were completely blindsided. No time to get their field heaters set, or plastic protective coverings in place. Heck, those guys couldn't even get their jackets zipped up quick enough to go look. In a matter of hours, everything and everyone was soaked to the bone, blown sideways, chilled numb, with extremities frozen stiff and hard as lollipop sticks.

There appeared to be only one exception to all this, on account of my arrival into the world on the first afternoon of that weather system. Mama would later say that she was the only one in town burning hot. Sweating up in the master bedroom like a call girl in a confession booth.

"It's time," Mama groaned to Daddy, who promptly left her bedside before things got a little too messy.

Mama must have taken her cues from the weather, 'cause just as the thunder and lightning kicked into high gear, her shrieks escalated to an ear-piercing crescendo. One last heave, and there I was.

"It's a girl!" our midwife, Mrs. Willis, screamed at the sight of me. "Finally, she's got herself a girl!"

Years later, I heard the various renditions of what happened next. That, in Mrs. Willis's great enthusiasm, she threw the sheet up so high, it flew over Mama's sprawled-out nakedness, then tucked itself completely around her exhausted head. When Daddy burst into the room

4

and saw his wife's head cloaked in white, after all those piercing cries from both Mama and Mrs. Willis, he just knew something had gone terribly wrong, that Mama must have died from the sheer act of trying to relieve herself of me.

"No, Eva." Daddy slumped his head to cry.

Mama would laugh herself silly for the rest of her days when describing how she sat up in bed, still covered head to toe and looking like a mummified corpse coming back to life in a Sears and Roebuck sheet set. Just then, a huge shot of thunder cracked across the sky, sending Daddy backward in shock, stumbling, and falling flat on his behind.

Little did I know, but that very second, I already had five older brothers laying in wait up the hall. Conniving together in their sloppy, smelly little rooms stacked with bunk beds. They were especially busy that day, thinking up tortures and torments to last the better part of my childhood. First thing on the list, my name. They were itching to give me a crazy name, something so wild and strange that maybe, just maybe, it might have begun to make up for my nerve, having been born a girl after the long running streak of Countryman boys.

"We promise to never complain about having a little sister"—John did the talking for them after they'd ventured down the hall to peek in Mama's room—"if you let us name her Snake."

"Or Lizard Guts!" James squealed as they burst into laughter.

"Nice try, boys. Now, get. Let me rest."

Mama was in no mood. Ready only for her marinated Tucks pads, a sitz bath, two aspirins, and a cup of chamomile tea. Five births under her belt before mine, and I'd still managed to make her feel like she'd just passed a piano through a porthole.

The wet afternoon intensified. The boys finally settled on a new name.

"Stormy!" they announced at her bedroom door.

"On account of the weather!"

Mama shuddered. "It sounds like the name of one of those beatniks over in the Bay Area."

"We could call her Elizabeth," Daddy suggested. "After my mother."

Mama patted his hand and held her tongue for as long as she could. "How about Faith?" she finally asked.

Daddy repeated it a few times. "It's pretty enough, but awfully religious, don't you think?"

Mama frowned. "You do realize that you sit in a pew every Sunday, don't you, Tom? And that our sons are named after nearly half of the twelve disciples?" Then she deftly played her card, giving him her sweetest smile and her most surrendering sigh, just like she did when Daddy came after her on Saturday nights.

"Faith Countryman," Daddy proclaimed.

Once in a while, someone would tell me that all of my strong believing must have come from my name, given that dark and chilly day in the middle of a ten-gallon cloudburst. Years later, Mama showed me its definition straight off the pages of the Holy Bible. It read, "The evidence of things unseen."

I was six days old when the morning sun finally sprang up to cast an eerie winter's radiance on our wet community. Normally ripe and rich with a variety of agriculture, our area had turned into a big ugly mess. Lagooned and reservoired. Puddles stagnant, souring the air. But lo and behold, our ranch had held ground, completely sustaining itself. In what appeared to be astonishingly admirable form. The whole place had weathered the storm by opening its mouth wide, taking in what wetness it deemed necessary, then spewing the rest onward in Daddy's remarkable drainage system. And to think everyone had shaken their heads, wondering why Tom Countryman was wasting his time on such a ridiculous project in the first place. Mama went so far as to call it the most productive male midlife crisis in the history of California ranching. There he was, day after day, for eight years, digging up faulty drainpipes and putting in new, tunneling underground, section by section. With nearly scientific splendor, he aimed it all for the big empty creek bed south of our land.

During his efforts, Mama assumed that Daddy was out there killing time, trying to get the heck away from her and the boys. Those were the longest days of Mama's life, when my unruly brothers peed on the floor for no reason but to watch it stream through the air in a nifty little arc, or they got their thrills jamming uncooked kidney beans up their noses, holding farting contests, capturing live tarantulas, and whatnot.

When that incredible storm hit, everyone suddenly realized that our father had done a spectacular job, especially in the drainage department. Others nearby didn't fare so well. The Sniders lost a year's worth of pearl onions and wound up on food stamps. The Pattersons' lima beans turned brown under a mucky pond. Daddy's friend Ralph Charleston agonized for weeks over his dead chickens, then finally shot himself in the head while his wife and kids shopped at Kmart.

It was a deluge of water no one would ever forget. As it turned out, I became a girl partial to rainstorms. I loved everything about them. Watching the sky darken to various shades of lead. Breathing in the smells that settled on the ground. Hearing watery taps across the roof, dripping off the edges.

Whenever the rains came, I'd get out under them. The warm rainfall of late summer was, by far, my favorite, though quite a rarity in the dry heat of our valley. Several years would pass until it returned, the cool wetness cutting through the stifling air. Those were the moments I felt most alive, as time slipped back and forth, and I celebrated my birth beneath a waterfall.

∼

I certainly don't remember that first gully-washer of a day when my family members discussed my name. But by age four, my eyes had opened with brand-new revelation, and clarity hit me square in the face, as I beheld everything and everyone in my world. There was Mama, with hair like dark honey, who spent hours on end in the kitchen, always looking her best, even on days she wouldn't set foot past the mailbox. My five streaky-blond brothers, with enough ants in their pants to keep them moving all day, tripping and scrambling up Rumble Road. Orchards of crops. A sun that set fire to summer sky. Nights falling silky cool. A cockeyed door hanging off a shabby barn. Cornstalks swishing on the breeze. And Daddy, just a speck of color out there in the fields, but growing large as life when he sat at the head of our supper table.

Not to be overlooked was Daddy's beloved sixty-acre grape vineyard. He referred to those vines as his harem of fickle women, who flaunted their stuff out the side door. In summer, they fluttered brilliant greens, leafy-haired, zinfandel-eyed, with clusters of fruit that dangled like costume jewelry. But come winter, they paralyzed in the fog and cold, their brown limbs crudely bent, gnarled and arthritic.

~

When electronics and pop culture collided together at the Countryman house, I observed a day like none other as my parents proceeded to dump Daddy's hard-earned ranching money down the drain with the purchase of a brand-new television set with rabbit ears on top.

We stood in awe, watching as he unloaded it from the truck.

"Now, before you go thinking we're getting all worldly here," Mama was quick to say, "just know that your dad and I bought this TV for two very good reasons. First and foremost, for the Reverend Billy Graham, whose crusades are broadcast every summer. And second, for Jack LaLanne, with all his robust physical fitness."

Under his breath, Daddy added, "Hmmph, that exercise nut who walks around in a leotard sucking in his stomach all the time."

During Billy's next televised sermon, Mama sat with her Bible opened, clenching a wad of Kleenex, her fingers locked in prayer position. Halfway through, she dropped to her knees and cried out loud.

"Faith, don't you worry now." Mama wiped her nose. "What you're seeing right here are tears of joy."

Things were altogether different when Jack LaLanne's physical fitness show was about to begin. Mama suddenly emerged from the bedroom decked out in pedal pushers with a matching pixie band. She pushed back the furniture, and started breathing real hard with a crazy look on her face, like she might bolt out the back door and sprint all the way to the canal bank.

Sometimes, though, it was just too much for her. The ranch, the endless chores, the five boys and snoopy little towheaded girl. One such day, Mama just stopped dead in her tracks while mopping dirty footprints off the linoleum for the umpteenth time.

"Kids?" Her voice quivered. "Did I ever tell you that, back at North Hollywood High School, I had cashmere sweaters in every color?"

We didn't know cashmere from cat food, but I quickly deducted that she didn't look so well.

"Mama, are you gonna try telling us that those right there are tears of joy, too?"

It was late in the day and Mama looked as tired as ever, just staring through the window. I watched her face when she spotted Daddy outside. He looked exhausted, too, pushing the wheelbarrow back to the barn. Mama finally took a deep breath, and some life came back in her eyes, and the mop started sliding across the floor again. Before James stepped in to finish the job for her. While Matt quietly put the dishes away. And Little Tom took out the trash.

Usually, though, our mama was a talkative creature, whereas my daddy barely made a peep. Probably on account of those ninety acres outside our door that worked Daddy to the bone from the first light of morning until well into evening. But I loved it when he was in a light-hearted mood, and he took me along with him on rounds at our ranch.

"Hold on, Faith!" he called out the truck window as I sat against the wheel well in the open bed.

Stopping in the orchard, he jumped out to pick a peach. "Here, taste this one."

"It's good." I chewed the fruit. "Real good."

Then he shushed me quiet. "Ya hear that? That's the sound of growing."

He and I stood under that peach tree for the longest time just listening to a bunch of silence. Until finally the train whistled by.

Daddy came from North Hollywood, too. Back when Mama had cashmere sweaters in every color, Daddy was pretty much wearing the same rolled-up Levi's and T-shirt every day, living in the middle of the orange groves near Lankershim Boulevard. He was from salt-of-the-earth folks. A family of ranchers, Baptist missionaries, and Sunday school teachers, with a couple car mechanics thrown in. Mama's people lived on the cashmere sweater side of town, where her father worked for a motion picture studio in Burbank. On any given day, Daddy's relatives could overhaul your transmission, save your soul, and recite the books of the Bible from perfect memory. Across town, Mama's family could tell you exactly what John Wayne ate for lunch in the studio commissary.

There was a saying for what Mama did when she fell face-flat in love with Tom Countryman. Some folks called it *marrying down*, but Mama never would have said so. After lovey-dovey vows in a hushed church full of white gardenias, she converted Baptist like Daddy, and they moved into his parents' house with only a little box of a bedroom to themselves. A few months later, a thick envelope arrived by mail, informing the Countryman clan that they were being given ridiculously short notice and absolute chicken scratch for compensation from the State of California, to hereby relocate and make way for the future expansion of the Hollywood Freeway.

That was when Grandpa and Grandma Countryman moved back to Minnesota. Mama and Daddy packed up their Bibles, cashmere sweaters, and Levi's and went north to Modesto. To invest in a piece of the earth before it was all snatched up. Daddy never did get over the memory of those beautiful orange trees being chewed and eaten alive by the earthmovers one hot summer in North Hollywood. He never stopped hating freeways either.

~

Despite the isolation of living on a ranch out in the boonies, come Sunday mornings, our family joined a big throng of people over at the First Baptist Church downtown. The boys put on their suits and fiddled with their neckties and rolled their eyes when they held the car door open for me. I shampooed and curled my hair and dressed in something Mama made with her own hands on the Singer. The best part was slipping on a pair of soft white gloves, with a tithing dime in the tip of the thumb.

One morning during Sunday school, I sat in a wooden chair, nibbling graham crackers, staring the whole time at a painting of Jesus knocking on someone's door. It was right then and there that my head opened wide and filled chock-full of the most amazing life-and-death information.

I learned all about our Lord and Savior, who at first almost sounded like a regular carpenter. Like Rob Robinson, who owned the cabinet shop on McHenry Avenue. But in the last few years of His life, when all those miracles started coming out of the woodwork, anybody with a clue figured out that this man Jesus was different. He spoke nothing but the most beautiful loving and saving and believing words you would ever hear. Later on, those words were printed bright red in the New Testament, so they could fly right off the page and hit you in the nose.

Around Easter, those Sunday school lessons grew serious. Like the day we heard that Jesus was killed, murdered on account of people's sins. Even people like me, who hadn't even been born yet.

"If you can accept these truths," our teacher explained, "and can concentrate on this one man's death, and pull love from Him into your heart, and mix it up with a bunch of your own love, well, boys and girls, you'll live forever."

A boy's hand shot up. "How long is that?"

"Forever and ever. Without ever coming to an end."

I squeezed my gloved fingers together, picturing the Son of God dying on a cross made out of sawed-apart tree trunks. His hands and feet pounded clear through with giant nails.

This living forever business sounded like a sure-fire good deal. There was only one hitch.

We had to *believe.*

No doubt, there were tougher things to do than to believe something. From what I'd seen of Daddy's life, getting up every morning at five a.m. to grow fruits and vegetables out of a dry brown earth seemed pretty hard. Mama had her challenges, too, turning five bratty little troublemakers into normal human beings. To believe in something seemed almost too simple.

Under brilliant summer skies one Sunday, the seeds of my beliefs were planted and they rooted deeply down. No doubts, hesitations, or waverings, I became utterly convinced that two thousand years ago, on a Friday afternoon, Jesus sacrificed Himself for all mankind. But before the darkness fell and the earth shook, before the Temple curtain ripped in two and the Old Covenant fell by the wayside, there existed a speck of time for every last one of us. Somewhere in a small fraction of a millisecond belonging to Faith Countryman, He took on death for me. For my sins and sicknesses. For my entire life with all of its joys and failures. Forever and ever.

That was it. The very manner in which the Son of God left the carpentry business, in order to save all the believers in the world from Hell and damnation.

Hallelujah.

~

So, the night it really all began, my brother Peter was six, and he was rolling around in his bed with a fever slung-shot up to 103 degrees. Sick enough to scare Mama over the edge in a way us kids had never witnessed.

"We've got to take him to the hospital, Tom. Now." She was wild-eyed, going nose to nose with Daddy.

But a hospital was where Daddy's mother had gone to die in a silver bed on wheels with plastic tubes clear up both her nostrils and one leg. Whether Daddy was remembering that, or calculating doctors' fees, or just tired, he wasted no time pulling Mama into the bathroom to whisper behind the door.

Creeping into my brothers' room, I sat next to Peter on the bed, instantly hot from being in such close proximity to his warm little body. His face was flushed, and his ears were bright pink and soft.

"Look at me, Petey." I held his shoulders.

Two gray slits appeared between his lids.

With a cool breath, I blew on his face and cupped my hands from his eyes to his chin. "Okay, enough of this, Petey. You're making Mama sicker than you. Come on. We'll just do this like Jesus did. We'll command it!"

Peter frowned.

"Be healed," I whispered.

The two gray slits opened.

"Be healed!" I repeated louder.

A chill shot through me, and it drove my head back. All I could think about was God, who must have loved Peter like crazy. Well, honestly, who wouldn't? With his two cowlicks and a hundred freckles, he was cute as a bug. I shut my eyes and remembered how Jesus was nailed to a cross for sin and death and disease. I concentrated on the very millisecond that belonged to Peter Countryman.

By the time Mama and Daddy stepped out of the bathroom, they found the two of us sleeping side by side on Peter's little bed with the cowboy sheets and red bandana pillowcases. His eyes were closed. Mama pressed her lips to Peter's forehead, and then to mine. Both of us were exactly the same temperature. Peter's fever had completely vanished.

~

Daddy may have despised freeways ever since North Hollywood's orange groves were gobbled up alive by them. Not us kids, though. We were nuts about riding up the 99 in the truck bed, watching the countryside shoot by. We always stayed on the lookout for hay trucks, because seeing one or passing one meant a free wish. Anytime those bales were spotted, we instantly hollered and made our wishes.

I doubled-down during the wishing process, with fingers and legs crisscrossed, my eyes shut tight.

"This isn't a prayer session, Faith," Little Tom yelled through the wind.

Poor Little Tom. He had two serious burdens in this world at the age of thirteen. An overbite that rivaled Bugs Bunny, and the same name as our daddy, Tom Countryman, which caused ongoing confusion in family conversations.

"This hay truck thing is just a stupid superstition," my eldest brother, John, stated loudly, holding his hair out of his eyes. Now into high school, he spent most of the time acting too big for his britches.

"It's like blowing out the candles on your birthday cake," announced Peter, who'd just blown out twelve of them two weeks prior.

As for me, I was absolutely elated when it came to hay trucks. And what a thrill to live in a place where such things were a dime a dozen.

"There's the fourth truck today!" I cried out. "Aren't we the luckiest? I can't even think of another wish!"

"You're so dumb." Matthew rolled his eyes. "Maybe if you had a brain, you could think of one."

"Yeah, maybe you should wish for a brain," Little Tom said as he snorted.

Okay, there were a few things from the Montgomery Ward catalog. Specifically, a transistor radio and a secret agent spy kit. But mostly I wished for things you couldn't buy, 'cause even with hay trucks up the 99 all day long, extra money at our house was tighter than a gnat's butt crack. So instead, I wished that Matthew's queasy stomach problems would subside. That John would get that job at the Chevron station. That my parents could afford braces for what Mama referred to as Little Tom's dental dilemma, with his four unsightly buckteeth pointing straight for the next county.

Lastly, I wished that my brothers could find it in their hearts to cut me some slack a little more often. Sometimes, their teasing was sheer torture. And despite me being churched-up real good, there were plenty of times I wanted nothing more than to line them up and kick them in the gonads, one after the next.

After our hay truck wishing ride, we tromped through the kitchen.

"Five hay trucks today," John announced to Mama.

"Hay everywhere," Little Tom added.

James joined in. "You could smell it coming from a mile away."

I was the last one in. "I ran out of wishes again," I whispered.

"Lucky you." Mama smiled down at me. "A girl who runs out of wishes already has everything she wants."

~

Lucky me, indeed, because immediately not one, but two of my wishes were granted. Both were manifested days later by way of the great American pastime.

Years earlier, when it dawned on Daddy that he'd bred an entire infield of sons, he built a genuine baseball diamond in an old grazing meadow. Nothing fancy, just a red-dirt plot of flat land, with feed-sack bases, a slightly elevated pitcher's mound, and a backstop made from scrap fence and barn wood.

Summer after summer, my brothers played for hours on end. Always without me. They made it clear I wasn't invited to participate in their games.

But all of that changed one sweltering day when two of the cool kids from school, Tag Barone and Chuckie Stocks, were visiting. Out of what must have been utter desperation, my brothers suddenly decided they needed another player. Moments later, there I was, clueless and athletically challenged, standing out in left field, holding my breath, wearing a big floppy glove missing most of its laces.

I couldn't believe my great fortune. I was actually being included in their game. It might have gone down as one of the best experiences of my life, except that my brothers chose to be even more generous by allowing me a turn at bat. When my big moment came, I slung the heavy wooden bat over my shoulder, stepped up to home plate, and turned to see Little Tom eyeballing me from the pitcher's mound.

"Just strike her out and get rid of her," James called impatiently from first base.

Squatted behind me in the catcher's gear was John, who must have felt some pity. "Eye on the ball, Faith," he softly spoke. "Then just swing the bat."

Well, who on earth would have ever guessed that I could actually hit a baseball? And with such unexpected strength! Or that the type of hit I happened to crush to smithereens would have its own name. The comebacker. Or that Little Tom, on the mound with his mouth hanging open, would have stood no chance of being ready for it.

Every one of us screamed our lungs out as the ball ripped from the meat of the bat and ricocheted to its original point of release, straight into Little Tom's face. It knocked him in the mouth, blood spurting everywhere, and laid him out flat on his back.

Holy spitballs!

We were now in some serious trouble. And I was in the biggest pickle of all, which, wouldn't you know, turned out to be an actual baseball concept. Our visitors, Tag and Chuckie, were sidestepping toward their Stingrays, as if planning a getaway. Matthew, with his weak stomach, hunched over third base on his hands and knees and retched on the bag.

I was the first one to fly to Little Tom's aid. And to a spectator it might have appeared that I was trying to slide into the pitcher's mound, which even I with my limited baseball knowledge knew was a dumb move. In truth, I had dropped down to glide to him on my knees for a very specific purpose.

My whispers began quietly, under my breath. "Wake up, Tom. Be healed, Tom. Perfect face. Beautiful teeth. Amazing smile. In Jesus's name."

The boys quickly gathered around us.

John called out, "Matt, quit barfing. Go get Mom!"

Suddenly, to our astonishment, Little Tom sat straight up. He leaned forward and coughed out every single one of those four protruding teeth from his mouth into his glove, roots and all.

Tag Barone was the only one who dared to look at me. He tugged my arm. "Hey." When I didn't respond, he tugged again. "Hey, Babe Ruth." He smiled. "Don't worry, he'll be all right." He pushed his dark hair off of his smooth brown forehead and grinned.

There was no pretty way of describing how Mama took the news. She leaped off the porch, shrieking to high heaven, sprinting to the rescue on legs toned by Jack LaLanne. We watched in amazement. She was into what we called her Spanish period. Hair dyed by Lady Clairol, side curls like a senorita's, listening to Herb Alpert and the Tijuana Brass all hours of the day. Even that very moment, "Spanish Flea" trumpeted out the window into the peach orchard.

My mother, brothers, and I carried Little Tom into the house and settled him on the sofa. Mama turned off the hi-fi, which by then had begun to drone out a depressing "Lonely Bull." We stared at Tommy's sunken-in mouth, minus the jutting bonelike enamels lined in his upper gum.

"Oh, sweet Little Tom." Mama tried to remain calm. "And you had such cute choppers!"

Cute? I'd never seen a kid more desperate for an aggressive workaholic orthodontist.

"We'll just tighten our belts, Little Tom," Mama said cheerfully. "And we'll get you some good false teeth. Or dentures. Or whatever they call them for boys your age. Don't you worry."

By the time Daddy came in, Little Tom's entire face was swollen and packed with ice bags. I was at the stove, making a clear broth for him to suck up with a straw. The boys were trying to be quiet and not get in Mama's way. She had the local yellow pages and her personal phone book spread across the table. For hours, she'd called dentist offices, friends, and even a couple of senior citizens without a tooth left in their heads, inquiring down to the most minute detail about the seriousness of Little Tom's predicament. And of course about the cost of four nice-looking false teeth. She was warned that the good ones were quite pricey. The less expensive options were not nearly as comfortable or cosmetically appealing.

For days, Mama dragged Tommy from one dental establishment to the next, hoping for a reasonably priced answer. Every night, Daddy gave the same advice. "Do what you gotta do, Eva. Just keep the cost down." Then Daddy would walk out of the room and Mama's chin would start to quiver.

After a long talk with Little Tom, my parents decided that, for the time being, whatever kind of fake teeth our regular dentist could conjure up would just have to do.

"For crying out loud, they used to make these things out of elephant tusks!" Daddy bellowed.

Mama looked incredulous.

Peter spoke up. "George Washington had teeth made of wood."

Mama started to cry.

In the end, Little Tom was bribed with gallons of Neapolitan ice cream, and when he was gorged fat and silly on the stuff, he was asked to think of this whole tooth matter as a temporary situation. Someday, in a year of good crop returns, Mama and Daddy would invest in the more expensive, nicer-looking false teeth made by the best prosthodontist in San Francisco.

But whenever Little Tom slept on the couch with the ice pack melting on his face, and if no one else was around, I secretly lifted up my prayers over him. My fingers gently touched his swollen lips while I spoke softly, saying whatever I could think of, hoping to get this thing resolved as best as I could.

After one of my most earnest prayers, I spotted those four buckteeth we'd salvaged that day in the bottom of an empty jam jar on the side table.

"Personally, Little Tom," I whispered so he wouldn't wake up, "I'm glad that you're rid of those ugly things." I stood to leave. "In fact, hallelujah! How 'bout that?"

When the day came for Little Tom's appointment with the dentist, that boy woke up in a mood so sour, no one dared speak. Who could blame him? He was tired of everyone tiptoeing around, putting pity on him, acting fake and congenial all the time. He was sick of soft food.

Scared of the probability of weird-looking fake teeth for the rest of his life. To top it off, his mouth was killing him.

"My gums just hurt," Little Tom whined as he and Mama set out in the truck that morning.

"They're probably missing their old teeth." Mama sounded exhausted. "You know, like amputees with their phantom pain."

We watched them drive down Rumble Road.

An hour later, the dentist confirmed the most interesting fact. Something quite remarkable had begun to occur in the aching mouth of our Little Tom Countryman. After a thorough examination followed by X-rays, Mama was asked to sit down in a chair for the startling news that a second set of four adult front teeth were now ready to pop through Little Tom's bare gums. And this time those things were coming in straight as arrows.

∾

I never came close to wishing on a hay truck for that hand-me-down Baldwin piano that rolled into our home on my twelfth birthday. Daddy and John muscled the cumbersome thing against the dining room wall and flipped up the music stand just as a truck pulled up outside with the words "Mr. Piano" stenciled across the driver's door.

"Somebody order a piana tuner?" a burly man called through the screen. He flashed his Piano Technicians Guild membership card as if it was legitimate identification.

"Oh no," John said under his breath.

Mr. Piano got right down to business, making his adjustments to the Baldwin. "I won't fill you with poppycock, Mr. Countryman. There's been some abuse to this once-fine instrument." Mr. Piano paused, baton-twirling his tuning hammer through his fingers. "But with a couple more tunings in the next several months, I'll have you guys sounding like Carnegie Hall around here. Now, which one of y'all is the pianist?"

That very instant, everything went quiet. Or *al niente*, as a real piano player might have described it in bona fide musical lingo. And except for the guy with the Piano Technicians Guild membership card, all heads whipped in my direction.

"Faith," Mama began slowly in a strange hushed tone. "We wanted so much to surprise you, but since we're all here now . . . Happy birthday!"

Mr. Piano reached out to me with a handshake. "You got strong hands, little lady. You're gonna be a natural."

As if that wasn't bad enough, the next day, my parents burst into my bedroom with the announcement that they'd just signed me up for piano lessons from one of the sure-fire loony tunes in our community, Mrs. Lenita Sheridan. Daddy beamed from ear to ear, while Mama clasped her hands.

"Wow," I barely managed to whisper.

"Music is such a blessed thing," Mama said, as if she'd made that discovery all by herself.

Now, I knew enough about Mrs. Lenita Sheridan to discern that she could put a real spook on a kid. We'd all heard about her one iris that liked to travel across the white part of her eyeball and make a beeline straight for her nose. Some called it lazy eye. That was hardly the end of it. She also happened to have not one, but two scraggly-looking three-legged dogs. What sick things could have been taking place at her home to have left her with a gallivanting eye and two deformed canines?

But I wasn't about to disappoint Mama and Daddy, so off I went, pedaling my bicycle every Tuesday afternoon along the canal bank and across the railroad tracks to Mrs. Sheridan's home.

"Right on time, little Miss Faith Countryman!" Mrs. Sheridan welcomed me cheerfully that first day, her head occasionally bobbling back and forth to keep up with the excursions of her meandering iris. "In piano, my dear, you will learn that timing is critical!"

Her piano room was dark. It reeked of dirty three-legged dogs, dusty sheet music, and Vick's cough drops, which Mrs. Sheridan constantly chewed.

As it turned out, Mrs. Sheridan's instruction was brilliant, and I was soon hooked. Not that I possessed a shred of talent for the piano, but because I was so thoroughly entertained by this colorful woman.

In one of our earliest sessions, she played "Mary Had a Little Lamb" at least a dozen times, each with a different stylistic approach.

"Appasionato!" she cried, eyes shut as she practically swooned over the keyboard. *"Bellicoso!"* she growled, roughly pounding each key. *"Dolcissimo!"* At last, it was the sweet-sounding melody I remembered from my early youth.

Mrs. Sheridan taught with great emotion—note reading, scales, timing, cadence, application, and, above all, the true intensity of piano as an art form. Then off I went, on an absolute musical massacre, destroying every single tune, one right after the other. But somehow Mrs. Sheridan's enthusiasm was enough to keep me coming back.

As the years went by, Mrs. Sheridan and I became close, although any knack I might have had for the piano remained elementary, at best.

"I'm pretty horrible, aren't I?" I finally asked her one day.

"I would never call you horrible, dear, but perhaps somewhat uninspired." She turned on the bench. "Faith, I'm going in the kitchen to pour us some iced tea while you sit here and think about what truly inspires you."

When she returned with the tea, I was already in the middle of it. The hymn was called "It Is Well with My Soul," and I was attempting it for the first time ever, by ear, perfectly, with chords precise and notes correct, sounding like an advanced student, one with genuine ability, as if I'd played this instrument since the day I was born.

Mrs. Sheridan paused in the doorway, looking thoroughly dumbfounded. *"Amoroso."* Tears gleamed in her eyes when I finished. "That was more than inspiration, dear. That was love." She sank into a chair across the room. "How did you do it?"

"I don't know. I just remembered the melody from church last Sunday, and out it came."

We remained silent for a few minutes, sipping our teas, sharing her Vick's cough drops.

Finally, she shook her head. "Church, huh? I've never been a churchgoer myself, but that playing-by-ear you just pulled off is enough to make anybody believe in something."

That next week, Mrs. Sheridan answered the door in a new pair of eyeglasses. Her weak iris appeared properly aligned at last.

Things never did change much with my formal piano training. I experienced very little progress, and dumped several music books, and even one metronome, on the floor out of frustration. But when it came to emulating a tune by our organist from services at the First Baptist Church, I was a regular Beethoven.

It was years into our friendship before I asked Mrs. Sheridan about her dogs. She explained that the younger of the two had been hit by a car, and that his leg was amputated in order to save his life.

"This other pooch still has his fourth limb." She reached down and gave the paw a yank, which caused the dog to yelp beneath the bench. "But ever since the other's accident, he keeps it tucked up under his backside."

"Why on earth does he do that?" I asked.

"For compassion and comfort and healing. Friendship." Mrs. Sheridan looked at me warmly through her shiny new eyeglass lenses.

Before I realized it, I'd lifted my fingers from the keys to throw my arms around her in a bear hug.

≈

In the late autumn of my thirteenth year, our valley sizzled with Indian summer. The mercury cranked up. The area dried to a crisp. Then one doozy of a brushfire began, ignited by some firebug on an arson spree.

That was exactly when my friend Weston La Rue lost his house and a whole stable full of horses.

As evacuations began, Weston's dad turned on the hose, climbed on the roof, and refused to leave. "No arsonist punk is gonna force the La Rues outta their home!" he shouted at all the neighbors driving away in their jam-packed station wagons. Like a hose-wielding gargoyle, he remained perched atop the shingles as the sky filled with ashes and the fire licked closer.

In the end, a concerned friend telephoned the La Rues to ask if they'd happened to look out their back window recently. Mrs. La Rue dropped the phone to go see, and she never did come back on the line. Turns out they didn't even snatch the car keys, they were in such a rush. Off they ran for their dear lives, holding the hands of the kids, leaving behind all the horses to snort and panic and kick like mad at their stall doors.

Those horses were really something, too. Beautiful creatures. Sinewy, with dark shiny coats and manes that rippled. Weston often showed me their pictures at school, always inviting me to go for a ride.

"Come on, girl. I want to take you on the ride of your life."

Whoa! Now, that was some serious cowboy talk! But a few months before the fire, I had finally accepted his invitation, because he was kind and dark-haired handsome and, without debate, the cutest boy in my grade. We loped through his property's back acres, and in the middle of a patch of shady trees Weston pulled me down from the stirrups to movie-star kiss me. So tenderly. *"Tenerezza,"* Mrs. Sheridan would have proclaimed, had she peeked her lazy eye at us through the thicket.

I liked that kiss. My first kiss. I liked Weston. I liked how his thick, inky bottle-brush eyelashes flapped up and down when he talked. I liked his persistence.

Two days after that catastrophic blaze wiped out their property, the entire La Rue clan was piled up in one room at the Motel 6, without a single car or horse to ever leave town on. Their house was declared a total loss by some guy in a shiny suit from the insurance company. No big shock there. You couldn't expect people to live in a pile of soot with the aroma of dead horses out back. With nowhere else to go, they rode the train to Colorado to live with Weston's aunt for a while. To get their feet back on the ground. Their legs knee-deep in an early surprise snowfall, too.

Weston sent me a postcard, telling me all about it. He scribbled, "I can't believe I'm a million miles away from you now. You had lips made for kissing, girl."

I laughed out loud when I read it.

But inside, a fiery block of heat shifted and rose.

~

Out of nowhere one chilly spring afternoon, Mama cornered me in the kitchen. "Faith, let's have a little talk."

At fifteen years old, I could only wonder what lecture Mama had up her sleeve this time. I quickly glanced outside. Daddy and my brothers were in plain view in the peach orchard. I watched them shuffle trunk to trunk, examining tiny blooms on our newly flowering trees.

Mama poured two cups of hot chocolate and leaned back in her chair. "Faith, honey, do you remember when all five boys had the chicken pox at the same time and I almost committed myself to the loony bin?"

"Who could forget that one? It was like being in a bad science fiction movie."

"There you were, right in the middle of it all. You didn't even get one pock, right?"

"Right."

"And then John had the roseola, and Little Tom had tonsillitis. There was Matt with his migraines, not to mention all his stomach issues. Peter's fevers, colds, and sinus problems. James, with the contact dermatitis and acne. Poison oak all around every summer for everyone."

I nodded.

"Except you."

I waited.

"How 'bout that horrible phlegmy flu three years ago?" Mama asked quietly. "The one that laid us all on our keisters."

"Yep."

"All but you." Mama eyed me from across the table.

I sipped my cocoa.

"Faith, you've never been sick. Not once."

She was right, of course. I'd never had so much as a headache, a cold, a menstrual cramp, or a charley horse. I'd never taken an aspirin, or used an ice bag or a hot water bottle. Our pediatrician often remarked that I was something of a phenomenon.

"I did get that bee sting that one time on the back of my arm," I offered cheerfully.

"That doesn't really count. Besides, remember when we looked an hour later? Sweetie, there wasn't even a red dot to prove it had ever happened."

I looked out the window. Little Tom had forgotten about the peach trees and was now chasing James. Both were laughing and tripping as they lumbered in the dirt, slowed down by their heavy boots.

"And not only do you never get sick, Faith, those around you seem to get well very quickly after you've spent any amount of attention on them."

I looked at Mama.

"Faith, I think we're gonna have to enroll you in Spiritual Gifts class at church."

"What? Why?"

"It's our best chance of finding out what's really going on with you!"

There was no use fighting Mama, particularly on church matters. "Spiritual Gifts class, huh?"

"The Lord's work," Mama pronounced in her most solemn voice.

So, one week later, there I sat, on a sofa in the library of the First Baptist Church with a dozen other students.

"Now, don't go getting yourselves into a panic about all this." The instructor, Mrs. Morris, waved her Bible at us. "Spiritual gifts are things you were already born with. They are your God-given, built-in abilities and talents. Things like teaching, evangelizing, compassion, encouragement, healing, miracles, prophecy, speaking in tongues, leading, and serving." Mrs. Morris winked at me from the podium. "Got it?"

"Yes, ma'am," I softly answered.

"First item of business in Spiritual Gifts class. A pop quiz." She winked again and passed out a thirty-page test. "Answer these questions as best you can, and that will lead you straight to the heart of your gift."

For all her winking, Mrs. Morris and her thirty-page test sounded dead-dog serious. As if I was applying for a job position that could last through eternity. One look at the quiz on my lap, then another at the door, and I wondered if chickening out and making a run for it might be my actual spiritual gifts.

As I focused on my escape plan, a man appeared at the door. It was the church janitor, Mr. Charles Bump, or "Bumpy," as everybody called him. He was tall and so skinny, he didn't begin to fill out his gray janitor's jumpsuit. The thing you'd never miss about Bumpy was the fact that he had the worst case of hiccups anyone in Stanislaus County had ever heard of. They were nonstop. Constantly interrupting his speech, his breathing, his eating and sleeping. Mama said he was now going on twelve years of those involuntary contractions. Mrs. Bump had even telephoned the Guinness World Records people about it, but lo and behold, they had reports of some guy worse off than Bumpy, hiccupping since 1922. Poor Bumpy: with all his suffering, he couldn't even make the record book.

"Pardon me ... Mrs. Morris ... hic ... for the interruption to your class ... hic ... but ... hic ... I'll be heading home now and ... hic ... may I please remind you to lock ... hic ... the doors when you leave."

"Thank you for your kind reminder, Mr. Bump."

From the sofa, I took a deep breath, instantly realizing that the simple act of breathing deeply was a complete luxury for someone like Bumpy, who'd probably try, then choke and sputter right on top of his next hiccup. Twelve years of those noisy things spasming around inside his diaphragm, pushing air into his lungs? It was unacceptable.

I went out the door after him. Mrs. Morris kindly pointed her pencil in the direction of the restroom, assuming that was my intention.

"Mr. Bump?" I whispered in the hall several lengths behind him.

"Yes ... hic ... ?" His smile displayed the weariness of a long day spent cleaning the church buildings and its grounds. But his eyes crinkled up some joy at the corners. "Oh, hic ... aren't you the ... hic ... Countryman girl?"

"Yes, sir. I'm Faith Countryman." I felt the years of hard work in the thick grasp of his calloused fingers. "Well, Mr. Bump, we really have ourselves a problem here, don't we?"

"Excuse ... hic ... me?"

"Aren't you about done with this?"

"Hic ..." He frowned at me.

"Lean down here so I can put my hand on your Adam's apple."

Bumpy leaned. For several moments we stood very still. My hand rested on the lump that covered his trachea, as the little spurts of air shut his epiglottis again and again. The hush of my praying echoed quietly down the empty hallway.

All the while, Bumpy's hiccups continued.

"No more!" I said suddenly, loudly, shocking my own self. I opened my eyes to release my hold on Mr. Bump. "And I mean it, too!"

With that, I turned around and walked back into class.

Every week that followed, while I sat learning how our spiritual gifts glorify the Lord and edify the church, I watched Mr. Bump pass by, still hiccupping his insides raw, causing his entire upper body to lurch with each contraction.

Mrs. Morris yammered on about gifting. Before long, I learned that the gift of healing wasn't anything magical. Usually, it wasn't even miraculous, and it was a far different endowment than the gift of miracles. Diseases and sicknesses didn't always disappear right on the spot. Healings often took time and, on many occasions, a doctor's intervention or a pharmaceutical aid. The bottom line was that someone had to throw his or her faith out there. This person had to fill up so full of believing, they'd yearn for nothing more than to intercede on behalf of the sick, get the prayer prayed, then leave the rest to the Great Physician.

After months of reading and testing, it was time for what Mrs. Morris called the "holy hot seat." One by one, she took us into the quiet candlelit sanctuary for a private, confidential discussion of our test results.

"Well, Faith"—Mrs. Morris and I sat together on the wooden pew as she flipped the pages of my test—"it appears that you may be equipped with a very interesting gift, that of . . ."

"Healing," I finished her sentence in a whisper.

She looked up. "But you already know this."

I smiled. "You're not going to tell me to load up on hairspray and go on TV with all the evangelists, are you?"

She chuckled. "The Lord doesn't call us to wave our gifts in people's faces. Your passion for healing can be utilized in subtle ways, too. Perhaps you're simply being pointed in a unique direction."

I nodded.

"But if you are truly drawn to the sick and the hurting, you'll end up using that gift for God's glory someday, one way or another."

Through the wall of stained glass windows, we could see Mr. Bump outdoors, collecting his rakes and shovels, flipping on the walkway lights for the evening. Out of nowhere, the wind started up, shaking the leaves off the branches above him.

"Here comes the fall," I announced, thinking only of autumn approaching, and with no clue whatsoever how prophetic my words would become.

Mr. Bump told us later about his fall. He was balanced on a ladder rung, cleaning the gutters along the roofline of the Sunday school building. And wouldn't you know, it was one of those blasted hiccups that caused the whole thing. Bumpy's upper body jerked so violently with the spasm that he lost his balance.

Now, it might have been the sheer fright of the actual fall itself. Or the crash-landing flat on his back, knocking the wind out of his lungs with more velocity than any of his hiccups of the past twelve years. Either way, it was a physical trauma capable of curing one wicked case of incessant hiccups. With no one around to hold on tight to his big calloused hand, or call for an ambulance, Bumpy remained there on the ground for a very long while. Until he realized he was lying still. Still as a stone. In a quiet, restful way he'd not experienced for twelve years. With no abnormalities of the diaphragm. No closure of the epiglottis. Not one nasty little hiccup.

When he finally crawled to his feet, Bumpy dragged his bruised and stiff body to the parking lot. He started up the church van and drove straight to Rumble Road.

Mama called out, "Now, what on earth is Mr. Bump doing here?"

I immediately went outside to hear the news.

"You were right, Miss Faith. No more!" His words echoed mine from months prior. "They're completely gone." His eyes moistened as we shook hands.

Somewhere in our flowerbed, a bullfrog suddenly decided to let out a big croak. It was a sound so spasmodically familiar, we both laughed. I watched Bumpy's eyes crinkle as he smiled.

"I've been there, man," Bumpy murmured to the little amphibian as he headed back to the van.

~

I was well into my teenage years the memorable night that Peter brought home his new classic Mustang convertible. He swooped into the driveway, then slid right out of it without even using the door.

"Let's cruise McHenry!" he hollered.

Ten minutes later, all of us Countryman kids were on the Central Valley's biggest cruising avenue. Packed in like sardines, mind you. My brothers were grown men by then, and I was seventeen, on James's lap, crammed next to the door. It was a Friday night, warm and wonderful for riding in the open air in the breeze.

"Come on," James egged Peter on at a red light. "Let's see what she's got!"

Peter tapped on the gas and the engine revved.

Matt whistled and shook his head in wonder. "It doesn't get any better than this."

As if to prove him wrong, a carload full of girls pulled up.

"Hey, Peter," a pretty brunette gushed at him from behind the wheel. "There's a big barn party tonight, on Paradise Road, at the curve." She managed to flip her hair around without taking her eyes off of my brothers. "You guys wanna come?"

Completely stupefied, my brothers were unable to speak. The light turned green and the girls went left, laughing and waving.

"Oh, man!" Little Tom thumped his palm against his forehead. "Why didn't I get a convertible?"

At the next signal, we stopped again.

"Hey," a boy's voice teased from a nearby car. When I didn't look, he tried again. "Hey, Babe Ruth."

Well, if it wasn't Tag Barone, that real cute kid from our tooth-popping baseball game years back. He still had the dark good looks I remembered, along with eyes that could really linger on you awhile, and a smile that slanted to reveal beautiful white teeth.

"You still slamming it out of the park, Faith?"

Now it was me who couldn't think of a thing to say.

"Or you just aiming for your brothers' heads?" He nodded at Little Tom, and everybody chuckled.

Stuck at the red light, Tag opened the door and stepped out of the passenger's seat. He was well over six feet tall now. Leaning his elbows on Peter's door, he grinned at me in the backseat.

"Hey, is this new, Pete?" He whistled, scanning the Mustang.

Suddenly, the engines of a Camaro and a lifted Malibu competed for everyone's attention. Tag laughed, slapped the palms of a couple of my brothers, and then climbed back into his car. The light flashed green, and we all moved forward. Peter turned up the stereo, and the Eagles began to sing.

The car next to us caught up again. Tag smiled. But there was something else this time. A look in his eye that wasn't there back when we were young and swinging bats too heavy for us, laughing and running the bases, and throwing the ball around behind the barn.

∾

Once in a while, our whole world would dare to change right before our very own eyes. The year my brothers saved our ranch was one such time. When John, James, Matthew, Thomas, and Peter became known as come-through guys, the kind of men you could really count on.

"Those Countryman boys are good stock," people around town started saying.

"Decent young men."

"They saved their entire grape harvest when Tom was called away."

Saving anything, or anyone, was about the biggest deal ever. I learned this the day I watched our neighbor, Mrs. Hawkins, jump into an irrigation ditch, fully dressed, hair fixed fancy, and wearing a brand-new Timex. With a groan that originated from the very depths of her bowel, Mrs. Hawkins pulled her blue-faced, nonbreathing four-year-old daughter out of the water. Then she threw that child on her back and undertook the most correctly performed and fastidiously delivered mouth-to-mouth resuscitation you ever saw.

There was so much love in all that saving. Every breath Mrs. Hawkins blew into the little purple mouth. Each push upon her tiny chest with the exact pressure and timing necessary. Love. Finally, after upchucking a few cups of cloudy trench water, you better believe that girl began to breathe again. To live again. For her mama's sake. And for those of us keeping real quiet, standing on the sidelines in the mud, praying for a come-back-to-life miracle.

∽

Our big saving of the ranch wasn't nearly as dramatic as an innocent child's near-death. But love drenched every agonizing moment.

It all started with a phone call one evening during supper.

"Your father's sick!" Daddy's aunt Rosie shrieked to her only nephew. She was in Minnesota, about three seconds away from being completely deaf, and speaking loud enough to be heard by everyone at our table.

"Just try to get here quick, Tom."

The situation sounded grim. So grim that Mama refrained from her usual comment about Aunt Rosie not really needing a telephone with that robust voice projection of hers.

After the dishes were cleared, a lengthy discussion took place on what to do about the ranch. Daddy and John scribbled pages of chores for each of the boys. Then Daddy went upstairs to pack and to put on his church suit while Mama called American Airlines in San Francisco.

"I'd much rather be driving." Daddy pushed down, flattening his heavy jacket in the suitcase.

"In this weather?" Mama watched the rain pour outside. "I don't think so, Tom. And from the sounds of it, you might not have time."

No doubt, Mama was remembering the horrors of our one and only road trip to Minnesota in the station wagon several summers back. When the air conditioning went out and my brothers were long-haired and sweaty. When Daddy became utterly possessed behind the wheel, and in his obsessive rush, he refused all food and bathroom stops except for dire emergencies. It was nothing but "Here's a couple of cherry Lifesavers to hold you over," or "Just keep your legs crossed if you gotta go," and "Don't even think about drinking anything," for two out of the four days. Mama watched Daddy with her eyebrows pinched together, like she was in excruciating pain. Meanwhile, Daddy just stared at the road.

Everything came to a head when we made the unfortunate discovery that we'd driven off and left Matthew in the bathroom stall at the Conoco station in Omaha. Poor Matt and that sour stomach of his. So, go ahead and nominate us for the Worst Family of the Year award, because no one even noticed the kid missing for a good half hour, despite the sudden extra legroom in the back of the wagon.

Little Tom finally called over his shoulder from the backseat. "So, Matty, what'd you ever get for that Don Drysdale baseball card, anyway?"

Silence.

Mama gasped until she choked, and Daddy hung a category-five illegal U-turn right over the dirt embankment on the I-80. He was fit to be tied, but not nearly as upset as Mama. She aimed all her anger straight at Daddy, for leaving Matt behind, for being in such a deranged rush, for keeping us on pins and needles, starving and thirsting us to death, imprisoned in what was turning out to be a very ripe-smelling station wagon.

When we screeched to a halt at the Conoco, there was Matt. Sitting on the curb, with tears streaking clean lines down his grimy little face. Safe and sound, though, and a lucky duck, too, with a free bottle of Coke from the station manager. The whole ordeal was terrifying proof that some so-called vacations were simply not meant to be. To top it off, the boys came down with an intestinal flu on the return trip, so we more than made up for pit stops and bathroom breaks on our final leg of that journey.

The bottom line was that my daddy would have given his life to get home where he belonged. He'd have gladly gassed it all the way back to Rumble Road. Just to lace up his boots again. Just to walk on the dirt of his land under an open sky.

That's how much he loved our ranch.

~

Grandpa Countryman took his sweet time dying. What started out for Daddy as a few days in Minnesota ended up lasting almost three weeks. When he wasn't at the hospital at his father's bedside, he was closing up shop at Grandpa's little mechanic garage or helping Aunt Rosie box things up in their father's house.

Back home, the boys juggled college courses, jobs, and all of Daddy's work on the ranch. In the cold, they put the hopper on the tractor to fertilize. After rain, they disked, knocking the weeds from beside the trunks of the peach trees and out from under the grape vines. As temperatures rose, irrigation began, with well water coming through the main ditch into pipes that streamed each row. Every day, the boys drove observation routes in the wheel tractor to check on things, not wanting any complications while Daddy was away.

Any farmer will tell you straight out, it all comes down to the weather. Sometimes, the weather played downright dirty tricks, like when it brought on a warm spell that caused our grape vines to act like it was spring already, with tiny green sprouts appearing out of the canes. But the absolute farmers' nightmare was when spring was going along just as nice and normal as could be, and suddenly, on a freakishly cold night, a late frost blasted in from nowhere to drop a deep freeze on every growing thing.

That April, while my Daddy sat at his ailing father's bedside, our vines back home were about to undergo an icy shock, a nasty death from a frost so severe that all grapes in the immediate region would be good as gone.

The morning before, John could feel it coming. "Right here." He showed all of us the newspaper article. "It says we're getting a serious cold snap tonight."

John drank two cups of coffee, staring at the page. Then he told the boys to go get their coats on. They spent the whole day irrigating, which might've seemed crazy due to recent rain and chilly weather, but it was a good try, keeping things wet so they wouldn't ice up so much later.

But that night's spring frost was the worst in thirty-five years. The next morning, our whole vineyard looked like someone had taken a blowtorch to it. All the green shoots with tiny grapes were now completely black. John paced for hours while we watched and wondered what to do.

"You can't control the weather, John." Mama did her best to console him. "There was nothing more you boys could've done."

Daddy's heart would have split to pieces had he seen the sight. But his heart broke apart anyway, because his father finally passed, making it even more impossible to divulge the fact that his beloved vines with the baby grapes were now stunted, black, and dead. Daddy informed us that he would stay one more week for the services, and then as soon as Grandpa was in the ground, he was heading straight for the airport.

"See you in a week then, Tom," Mama said softly before she set the phone back in its cradle.

"Okay, you guys," John said to our brothers. "We've got exactly seven days."

During this time period, my brothers put everything else in their lives on hold, in order to hunker down and work harder than ever before imagined. Day by day, vine by vine, shoot by shoot, they snapped off the ugly black extensions left damaged by the frost.

Neighbors who'd already given up on their own vines parked at our fence, rolled down their windows, and offered their two cents' worth.

"Can't fight Mother Nature, boys."

"No amount of work, however well intentioned, will fix this."

But my brothers were relentless. Their gloved hands moved at record speed, covering sixty acres, snipping like madmen with farm tools, row after row, from sunup until the last bit of light. Until all their friends joined in. Until I did, too. Until Mama had us on hot-cooked meals three times a day. Until we cried out for relief.

"Frost to fruit," I mumbled as I worked. "Water to wine, baby." Dizzy and delirious, I only allowed myself to imagine the most glorious bushels of grapes.

Finally, the night before Daddy came home, every last one of those cotton-pickin' black shoots was finally hacked off, thrown in the truck, and dumped at the fill off Maze Boulevard.

~

There is not a soul on the planet who would've ever called it our best crop. But it was quite possibly the craftiest save in the entire county that year. We managed to harvest our whole vineyard, including our red seedless table grapes, with their unique pink-rose color and surprisingly sweet taste. We trucked hundreds of lugs back and forth to the packing shed after two separate pickings. We even squeaked out a third, of scraps, for filler wine that we dropped in the tub for crush at Bustiani Cellars.

My brothers did all the labor, but it was their love that saved our ranch. And it was only natural that love would come trailing after them, in the good way that it does when people have done the right things from out of the deepest places inside them. The girls who were looking for come-through boys started seeing my brothers in a different light. And these weren't the hair-flipping, ditzy girls looking for a party. They were the long-legged beauties with kindness in their eyes, and something serious and long-lasting on their minds.

~

That fall, as those resurrected-from-the-dead Countryman grapes ripened to their fullest potential, Tag Barone, with all of his country-boy charm, braked his pickup at the edge of our cornfield and made his way back into my life. Fresh out of high school, I had no clue that his arrival would bring me face-to-face with a strange and powerful force of nature. Something strong enough to send a good Baptist girl with the church-verified gift of healing to the mercy of one handsome, heartbreaking bad boy.

Lust.

When lust hit, it brought a fast-striking match, and I was burned in its firestorm. Years later, when I wished I'd never met Tag Barone, I'd always remember the look he gave me on the porch that day, if only to wonder what girl could've ever resisted.

It was a hot September afternoon when Tag showed up to sit on our porch swing, not bothering to ring the bell.

Spotting him through the window, I stepped out to greet him with a cool drink.

"It's about time." Tag grinned, standing. He gulped the icy lemonade, and propped himself against the porch rail. To say that his frame had filled out nicely was an understatement. His tanned arms rippled with muscles from the work on his daddy's farm. A stream of liquid slid down his chin and onto his chest. He wiped his mouth with the back of his hand and shot me a dazzling smile. "It sure is good seeing you again, Faith."

That Saturday night, Tag parked his truck next to the cornfield and climbed up our porch steps. He looked my daddy straight in the eye, engaged in lively conversation with my brothers, and rose to his feet when Mama walked in the room.

A few minutes later, he touched my arm. "So, Babe Ruth, you ready to go?"

For the umpteenth time, the story of our memorable baseball game was retold, with all the exaggerations the years had tacked on. Little Tom was as amused as anyone, and I couldn't help but notice his perfect teeth.

"You look great," Tag whispered to me as we stepped off the porch.

"You too," I responded.

"I mean it, Faith." He opened the truck's door for me. "Your blond hair with those blue eyes. Your figure. You're really beautiful."

On our first date, we ordered steaks at the fanciest restaurant in town. Our second date was going to the movie theater. By the third date, we were parked in his daddy's peach orchard, in the bed of his pickup with a six-pack of Budweiser. I knew it was illegal and sinful, or even possibly dangerous, to be doing such things. Drinking underage, all puckered up with a boy in the middle of nowhere. But I finished two cans and ended up kissing him until my lips ached and throbbed.

Until all the fires were lit.

A few days later, Tag and I were holding hands on the porch steps. When I ran my thumb along his knuckles, he quickly pulled away.

"What's wrong?" I asked.

"You don't want to touch these."

I saw that his hands were covered with warts. They dotted his skin with bulging whitecaps.

"Those warts right there? Oh, they're nothing," I assured him. "We'll get rid of them in a snap."

"Impossible." Tag looked down at his hands. "I've already tried every ointment there is at the drug store."

"I'll just pray them away." I smiled. "Save you some money, too."

"Pray them away?" He had an odd expression on his face.

"Yeah." I waved my hand in the air. "They'll be gone in no time."

"You mean, like pray . . . to God?"

"No, I thought I'd try the Man in the Moon this time. Then I'll sacrifice a chicken, drink its blood, and do a voodoo dance." I laughed. "Of course God. Who else does anyone pray to?"

Right then, I clasped his hands and shut my eyes tight to pray a prayer so quiet that Tag could barely hear my words. All the while, I stroked his warty viral knuckles.

"Amen," I finally whispered, and kissed him passionately on the mouth, certain that when I opened my eyes, Tag would be gazing at me as if I was an angel of mercy sent from the heavens. Instead, his cheeks were streaked red as he pulled free and rattled his truck key.

"I gotta go."

Tag walked to the cornfield and climbed behind the wheel, shaking his head every step of the way.

But like a fool, I smiled myself silly and waved him all the way down Rumble Road.

～

Weeks went by, and Tag didn't call. The best-looking boy in all of Modesto had officially dropped me like a hot potato. *"Al fine,"* Mrs. Sheridan would've pronounced from the piano bench with a solemn bow.

Who would've guessed that a simple prayer would send a guy running for the hills? Maybe trying to help the sick wasn't such a gift after all.

As expected, Mama brimmed over with words of wisdom from her perch at the kitchen sink. "Faith, there are lots of boys in this world." She was wearing rubber gloves and scrubbing the daylights out of a cook-pot. "Zillions of these Tag Barone types, too." His name sputtered out of her like a bad taste. "And most of them aren't exactly looking for a nice girl. At that age, they're usually tomcatting around, looking for one thing."

It didn't take a rocket scientist to know that *one thing* was a million miles away from praying for knuckle warts. That thing was parked out in Tag's truck after dark, in a peach orchard, with beer and kissing, and nearly going too far to ever come back home the same.

~

Time dragged on. No matter how bad I wanted to curl up in a ball to cry about my first boyfriend giving me the royal kiss-off, our family was smack dab into picking by then, plucking through rows like there was no tomorrow. After years of practice, I was able to go through the motions like an expert field worker, all the while pouting and pitying myself. I loosened the clusters, gently snipped them from the larger branches, placed them in the bucket, sighed heavily, then moved on to the next bunch. Memories of Tag rolled over and over in my mind. How good he looked drinking lemonade on the porch, giving me that look. How delicious his kisses tasted under the peach trees. *Hey, Babe Ruth*, I could almost hear him tease.

"Faith!" Mama shook the vine from the other side of the row. "Give it a rest, would ya?" She plopped down her bucket. "For crying out loud, good looking and built like a Greek god or not, the guy was infested with a bunch of ugly warts, okay? Those things are catchy, too. Hope you washed up after all that smoochy hand-holding you two were doing."

"I just wonder how I could've scared him off so bad." I blinked back tears.

Mama scowled. "You were too good for him, that's how."

"Yeah, right," I sassed sarcasm at her.

Mama grabbed my arm at the row's edge. "When a boy leaves you like that, you let him go. You hear me? Put him on a fast horse. Give it the whip. Turn your back and walk away. You understand, Faith? Let this one go."

~

When Saturday came, Peter and I were instructed by our parents to stop picking, pull forty dollars out of the coffee can, and take the truck to Pippy's Market for groceries. Perfect timing, too, 'cause just as we arrived, Tag Barone was coming out the door with a root beer.

Peter shook his hand and went inside with Mama's list.

"Hi, Faith." Tag's smile was killing me on the spot. "You're looking good, as usual."

I kept walking. "Thanks."

"You pickin'?"

"Yeah. You?"

"Yep. Heading back right now."

I stepped toward the door.

"Hey, Faith, let me show you something."

Tag held out his hands. Despite the fact that I was still hurt, heartsick, and madder than a wet hornet, I couldn't help myself from reaching out to touch them. Where just weeks before dozens of warts had bubbled, his skin was smooth and flawless.

"Wow."

"They were gone the next day." Tag watched me closely.

I looked at his face. "So were you."

"I was pretty freaked out. Sorry."

"Yeah." I took a breath. "Me too."

"What are *you* sorry for?"

"I'm sorry you didn't have what it takes."

"What it takes?" He eyed me curiously. "What do you mean?"

I turned to go. "For me."

With that, I did exactly what my mama told me. I snapped the whip down on Tag, and on that horse he rode in on, too. As Pippy's door slammed behind me, I let go of that handsome boy with his perfectly smooth hands.

~

But with a name like Tag, there was bound to be a chase. It turned out to be one hot pursuit, too, occurring right in the midst of intense valley heat, as again, we were tomahawked by a long-lingering Indian summer the likes of which we'd never seen before.

Just when we could barely stand another day, Modesto's most highly anticipated party of the year was thrown. It was the annual harvest festival, hosted by Angelo Bustiani, the area's most successful vintner, wine producer, and businessman.

Bustiani's three-story estate seemed a world away from our humble existence off of Rumble Road. Carloads full of guests arrived to stream through the gardens and onto patios, as sycamores swayed overhead. Servers splashed wine into goblets. Rich aromas drifted from an open spit. The place was alive in celebration.

Crossing a bridge over a shady pond, I sank into the catbird seat, a bench with a clear view of the entire scene.

As usual, Bustiani was the life of his own party. *"Salute!"* he toasted his guests, dancing with a circle of children who giggled until they fell over.

I glanced at the entrance. Tag Barone arrived. Except for the triple-digit temperatures, he was most likely the hottest thing around. I moaned under my breath, then watched the heads turn to get a better look at him. Girls my age. Older women. Everyone.

"Breathe," I reminded myself, and I continued to watch.

Tag shook a neighbor's hand. He squeezed his mother in a bear hug and greeted friends from school. Finally, he paused to gaze across the pond. Lifting his glass, he smiled at me until his father interrupted, pulling him into a nearby conversation.

Moments later, on my way back from the powder room, Tag appeared out of nowhere. Laughing, he pulled me into a dark paneled room and shut the door behind us. My eyes widened, working to adjust to the dim light. We were standing in a library, surrounded by bookshelves and heavy draperies.

"You got a sudden urge to read, Tag?"

"Not exactly." He pressed his mouth against mine.

I pulled back. "I don't think we're supposed to be in here."

He kissed me again, harder this time.

Seconds later, the dinner bell clanged outside the window.

"Okay, Miss Goodie Two-shoes." He laughed. "We'll go back out there."

After the meal, Tag caught up to walk with me along the cobbled pathway to the vineyard where the men congregated each year. They would spend the rest of the evening here, admiring Bustiani's acreage, smoking cigars, and telling stories.

Bustiani's arm hung around my father's shoulders.

"Look at that, Tag. My daddy's over there bursting with pride."

"He should be. He's the only one around who managed to cheat that frost last spring."

"Thanks to my crazy brothers." I laughed. "Your dad looks pretty happy, too, Tag. These guys really think grapes are everything, don't they?"

"Yep."

"And how 'bout you?" I admired him under the moonlight. "You gonna be a vintner like your daddy?"

Tag drained his wine goblet. "Oh, heck no. I'm outta here as soon as I finish JC this semester."

My mouth dropped. "Really?"

"Yep, I promised my dad a couple years of college before I go to LA."

"LA?" He might as well have hurled a medicine ball straight at my belly button. "As in, Los Angeles?"

"Yep."

"To live there? Just you?" Desperation cracked in my voice, and I wanted to bite my tongue to make it stop.

Tag straddled my legs with his, cupping my face in his hands. "To live there. Just me." He grinned and kissed my nose.

"Oh." My heart was beating madly. I wasn't sure whether I was hopelessly sad or incredibly ticked off.

"Yep." Tag paused. "I'm gonna be an actor."

"An actor!" I gasped. Not because he didn't look the part. He most certainly did. Come to think of it, there wasn't a single flaw on this guy. No wonder he was headed for Hollywood. Why, he'd storm right in and conquer the show business industry with that face and physique of his.

"My parents are pretty mad. They keep telling me to get a real job, but I don't want to work my whole life and make some other guy rich. Like him." He nodded at Bustiani. "I want to work for myself. I want to be the rich guy."

"Oh." A lump grew in my throat.

Tag pulled me back up the path. "You wanna come?" His voice sounded soft, Hollywood-actor soft, like the cameras had pulled in for a close-up, and the mikes were hot.

Did I wanna come? Where? Back up the cobblestone path to the party? Or all the way to LA to be a part of his plan?

But "mmm" was all I could manage to answer as he kissed me again.

I was still relishing the memory of Tag's kisses when I slipped into my bed that night. But I was choking on that lump in my throat, too. I should've said my prayers and confessed my sins. I should've called on all my dreams and unredeemed hay truck wishes. But I was exhausted and asleep before I knew it.

Lo and behold, the weather finally changed.

Then, as life would have it, so did I.

⌒

The tule fog rolled in thick and soupy with skies smeared murky gray out our kitchen window. Mama and I listened to the forecast on the radio as her special three-berry pie cooled on the counter. She and Daddy were headed to the county competition in Turlock that night, where Mama would likely win first prize for her baking again.

"Sure you don't want to come, Faith? Little Tom's bringing Farrah Fawcett."

Little Tom's prize pig had been fattening for months.

"Not this time." I watched her carefully sprinkle sugar on the lattice crust. "I bet you'll be coming home with another blue ribbon, Mama."

"You think so?"

"Definitely so."

"Wish you'd come along with us, honey." Mama smiled, carefully placing the pie in its carrying box. "Things just aren't the same without you."

But nothing ever stayed the same forever.

And while the Countrymans had a rule for just about every single thing under the sun, no one ever mentioned much about my honor, or a thing called resistance, or how a boy showing up unannounced at the back door on a cold night could somehow turn the road sideways on you.

But Tag had that perfect Hollywood movie-star face of his. He also had a confident smile that slanted easily across his teeth. By the way he looked into my eyes, he was either over-the-moon nuts about me or spectacular at pretending. I knew the latter was entirely possible now. After all, he was an actor.

Later, after Tag had gone home, I wasn't sure whether I should cry, sniffling all the warm berry smells of Mama's sweet kitchen up my nose, or run a mile down Rumble Road screaming "What have I just gone and done?" at the top of my lungs.

One thing was certain. My head was about to collapse under the weight of a zillion new thoughts. And whether you called it love, or lust, or something else entirely, it was a whole bunch of everything coming at you at once. And most definitely, it was something that could leave you feeling full as a bucket and empty as a drum at exactly the same time.

Or just lonely for that little girl you turned your back on, standing there in her Sunday Mary Janes and handmade dress, on the gravel road where she was born.

If only I'd known. If only I'd tidied up afterward. Scraped off the muck with some good old-fashioned repentance. But instead of prayers, my sorrows rose, ribboned with guilt, only to crash and burn on the wide-open field of faithless self-condemnation.

It was under these festering conditions that I prayed for a girl named Lacy as she lay suffering from complications of diabetes in a cold bed under fluorescent lights over at Meadows Hospital. I should have stayed away in my rebellious state with my distracted mind, but Mama asked me to pray, speak in tongues, and lay hands on the girl as a favor to Lacy's mom.

"Most likely she won't make it through the night," Mama explained. "But go and give it your best shot anyway, would ya?"

Whoa!

Needless to say, Mama's cup was not exactly running over with a bunch of white-hot faith. Come to think of it, she'd been nothing but lackluster with me for days. I'd catch her watching me with the strangest look on her face. It was as if she'd come home from the county competition with her blue-ribbon pie, and with one look at my guilty face, she must have known I'd changed.

I might as well have sassed her. "That's right, Mama. I did it. All over your kitchen floor, too. Better go get the mop!"

It just goes to show how detrimental things could become when a person wasn't spiritually called to a particular need. Or as was the case here, a radical healing in a hard-pressed, back-against-the-wall emergency. Because when that sweet Lacy girl left this earth by way of the Meadows Hospital ICU, she didn't just die like everyone else. She died holding my hand. Staring at my face. While I looked like a fool, busting my gut with guilty prayers, hoping like mad she'd somehow be able to live.

But Lacy's spirit departed, and when it did, that thing moved like an elevator on free fall to the bottom of the chute. I felt its shudder run straight through her body and out. Until all that remained was her empty little shell of skin and bones. And a bunch of red-eyed relatives standing around blowing their noses.

There were so many reasons to cry, but I did not have one single tear in my entire head to squirt through a tear duct. I tried. For some relief. I wanted to wail about everything that was dead and lost and changed. But all I could do was go back home, slump down on the piano bench, and play a song by ear that I swear I never heard before in all my life.

Mama came in from the clothesline with a basket of clean whites. "It wasn't your fault, Faith. I'm sure you tried your hardest. Lacy had a very serious illness. It wasn't like Peter's fever, or Little Tom's buckteeth, or Bumpy's hiccups." She carefully watched my face. "It wasn't like your young man's warts either." She started up the staircase with a stack of fresh towels.

My hands lifted from the keys. "Hey, Mama, you think ridding a man of a twelve-year case of hiccups was some kind of cakewalk?"

"I'm just saying, it's not like it was a real disease or anything."

"Oh yeah? Well, you go tell that to Mr. Bump, why don't you?" I shook my head, and pressed the chords. "Better yet, try telling it to the good Lord Jesus."

Mama stared at me, before continuing up the steps.

~

It didn't seem to matter one bit that I never really knew Lacy. The death of that girl pushed against me with such shame and despair that one week later in the middle of the night, Tag Barone parked his truck on our property. Not in his usual spot next to the cornfield, but in a dirt patch at the northernmost gate under a milky sliver of a moon. From there, he watched me drag my suitcase all the way across the dirt and heave it into the bed. Without lifting a movie-star finger, mind you. Which should've been clue number one of what would turn out to be hundreds. But then he sneak-previewed that smile he was taking all the way to Hollywood, so I just climbed into the seat beside him.

His truck started to creep along my daddy's property path as a train sounded on the rails. I'd heard that sound every single day of my life, the lumbering along the tracks, the screeching and whistling.

I was going to miss those trains.

"You ready for this?" Tag slowly made the turn on Rumble Road.

"Sure," I lied through my teeth.

I was about as ready for this as a cannonball off a cliff. As ready as hearing that train for the very last time. For seeing the house lights flicker on as we quietly drove past, imagining the letter I wrote in Mama's trembling hands while her little heart split to pieces.

~

Riding shotgun away from the only place I'd ever known, I started to weep, and with every passing minute my crying intensified. Those tears must have been stockpiled since the night the tule fog and Tag Barone both rolled in on me. Since Lacy died, leaving me with egg on my face, midsentence in a half-fake thinking-too-much-of-myself prayer of petition.

All the while, Tag chased the yellow line south.

Somewhere around Fresno, he and the entire Led Zeppelin band started climbing the Stairway to Heaven. Turns out, Tag was a devoted, if not possessed, fan, ready and willing to endure "Stairway to Heaven" in its entirety eight times in a row.

Peering over my wad of Kleenex, I studied him as he sat behind the wheel. Here was a man whose plans had recently escalated. Anxious and unable to wait any longer, he had decided to leave Modesto earlier than planned.

"Hollywood or bust!" he shouted, heading straight toward his destiny.

Then there was me. A puffy-eyed mess. Heading into Tag's destiny, too, while my own future dangled in the balance.

Who is this guy, anyway? Do I really know him or even love him?

"Oh, Tag, what am I doing?" I finally cried over the noise of the engine and the music.

Tag smiled and turned down the volume. "I'll tell you what you're doing. You're leaving behind a town full of nobodies and a big pile of nothing."

I closed my eyes.

"You're heading to the most exciting place in the country! I guarantee, you will never see anything like LA! It's a circus down there."

Tag performed a drum solo on the steering wheel, followed by an air guitar riff on his thigh. But after years of pulling my hair out, banging the keys and thumping the pedals over at Mrs. Sheridan's, I was of the belief that you didn't act like a musician unless you were a musician.

Oh, Mrs. Sheridan! What on earth would she say when I didn't come knocking on her door next Tuesday? What about Bumpy over at First Baptist Church, who always looked for me on Sundays to show me how quiet and unhiccuppy he continued to be? And of course, there was my family, but I didn't dare think about them.

Tag continued to pound the daylights out of the steering wheel while staring through the windshield. Lousy rock 'n' roll pretender or not, his profile was a stunner. He turned to flash me a smile. And zing! White teeth all over the place. Definitely ready for his Hollywood close-up.

Hours later, the freeway dipped off the ridge route and the sun lifted up a new morning. Below the dingiest skies I'd ever seen, Tag's truck rolled along the lanes of traffic that sank between the suburbs.

"Welcome to the San Fernando Valley!" Tag's excitement was uncontainable.

The Stairway to Heaven had taken us south. Then west. All the way to the Pacific Ocean, where the waves couldn't make up their minds whether to plop down and stay put, or pull up froth and go rolling back.

Go back. Go back.

I was still blinking on my tears when Tag picked up the keys to our apartment on 12th Street in Santa Monica, three buildings up from Wilshire Boulevard.

"This place was really something in its heyday," the landlord boasted, leading us down a hallway of tattered and stained carpet.

He opened the door to apartment 10 and flipped on the light. An army of cockroaches scurried for cover in the baseboards behind cigarette-stained walls.

I held my tissue against my lips to keep from screaming.

Tag walked in and went straight for the Southern California view. Whipping open the dirty drapes, he proclaimed, "I love it here already!" Beyond the glass, a few feet away, 12th Street was jam-packed with parked cars, palm trees, apartment buildings, and passersby. "LA!" he exclaimed. "Man, this place really is a circus!"

SANTA MONICA,
CALIFORNIA

~

If LA was a circus, what I witnessed every day on 12th Street was one big parade. Each morning, the procession began in the dark with a trickle of humanity rippling down the avenue. The homeless were always first in line, like sluggish drum majorettes on raggedy legs. Up and ready to starve to death all over again. To dream up stuff they'd give for a piece of bagel or muddy coffee.

My very first morning there, I met the man I would nickname Quarters. Because that's all he ever talked about. "Any quarters today, miss?"

Quarters had dreadlocks, but by pure accident, from lack of shampoo and a comb. He had some big vacuous eyes, too. They pulled me right in when I dropped the money into his filthy hand.

"Thanks, miss." Quarters counted the coins without looking, then veered back onto the parade route. The tops of his shoes were the only parts left, clapping down on the street all the way to Wilshire.

Quarters wasn't the parade's only regular participant, and even those who didn't sleep in cardboard washing machine boxes were sights to see. There was Malibu Barbie, with a body strategically built by designer doctors. There were the power walkers. The UCLA students.

The surfers, all continually stoned out of their minds. There was the crusty old lady next door, Mrs. Crackleberry, who carried her Salem carton around like it was clutch purse couture, who dragged on cigarettes till her cheeks went hollow, then flicked the ashes in her blouse pocket.

It took less than a day for Tag Barone to join the procession along the parade route, to begin moving in sync with everyone else. He gladly took his place. Freshly scrubbed. Handsome as all get-out. Walking to his truck each morning to drive to the big top in Tinseltown, to seek out the Hollywood agent who would discover him and make him a star.

There was a pungent smell in the air. It was the salty water of the Pacific pushing inland, greeting us at the door, following us inside, laying with us at night. But there were no dirt paths or back porches. No vineyards or barns. Not a single peach tree in sight. There weren't any trains rumbling against the rails either. Worst of all, I hadn't seen a single hay truck full of free wishes to get me out of this place to go back home where I belonged.

~

It took me five years to get my can filled and come to my senses.

The first thing to go was the sunshine.

I quickly discovered that it wasn't always so bright and cheery in Southern California. As a matter of fact, Santa Monica's fog banks habitually camped right on top of our heads, especially on mornings and sometimes for weeks on end. Whether I was working as a waitress at Westwood Café or running errands on Wilshire Boulevard, I often wondered if I'd seen the last of sunny skies. Then finally, a day of brightness would blast through the gloom with luscious warmth. Those days were honey gold, when everyone went outside, to the beach, to the parade route under the sun.

"Nice day, huh, Quarters?" I put coins in his palm as he folded himself in a quirky bow, bending clear over his bottomless shoes.

It was one of those sparkly afternoons when I sat on the steps to watch Mrs. Crackleberry puff by like a little smokestack. Suddenly, Tag pulled up in the truck with a big shout.

"I got an agent! A Beverly Hills agent! Marcy Steiner! She's one of the best!" He added with a sniff, "She's very well connected."

"Oh, Tag!" I cheered as he scooped me into his arms. "Now we're really going to see great things happen for you!"

"I'm supposed to call her two times a day, to check if I have any auditions."

Those two-a-days with the very well-connected Marcy Steiner soon became lengthier phone conversations. Who would've ever imagined that Tag could talk such a mean streak about headshots and callbacks and doing lunch? All the while posing in the mirror, running his fingers through his hair, pumping barbells, and clicking the television remote.

From our couch, I had the best seat in the house for those performances. And despite his enlarged ego run amuck, it was impossible not to marvel at how Tag had grown more hot and handsome than before. Turns out, LA did that to people. It was as if there was a rule, "Get hot, or get out of town."

As time passed, Tag grew oddly cold and distant. He began acting like a stranger, not at all like the boy back home who stepped off the running board, pushed back his hat, and knocked me over with his smile.

"Are you okay?" I handed him a cup of coffee one morning.

"Yeah, why?" He looked away from me out the window.

"You just seem, well, kind of different."

"I'm under a lot of pressure right now." He sighed. "It's not easy to keep the phone ringing, you know?"

"I know."

"Even Marcy's bugging me to get more work."

In no time flat, Marcy Steiner discovered that Tag Barone looked drop-on-your-butt amazing without a shirt on. She soon landed him a single-shot deal in *Playgirl* magazine. A cowboy-themed pictorial filmed in some phony-baloney horse stall, Tag reclining on a bale of hay. Not buck naked, just bare-chested. With the top button of his Lee's undone, to give the impression that he just couldn't be bothered keeping his fly completely closed.

Tag got other jobs after that. A couple of lines in a soap opera, the host of a kid's game show pilot, and a local commercial for a gym. A Bullock's underwear campaign, too, with print and commercial ads, a billboard that overlooked the Jiffy Lube in Culver City, and a lifetime supply of free briefs. It was always "any day now" that his big break was coming.

The second thing to go was the sanity.

Change swirled above us in the grayish-brown air. It was as if someone in apartment 10 had suddenly turned loose a bunch of rattlesnakes. Tag grew angry and miserable. Like so many others chasing their stars in Hollywood, he started drinking too much, smoking pot, and living on the verge between any day now and his big break.

"Okay, what's wrong with you now?" I finally asked one day as we walked along the parkway at Ocean Avenue, tired of dealing with his sullen moods.

"Eleven casting calls this month, and not one callback for a second look." Tag threw up his hands. "I'm beginning to wonder if I'm any good at this."

"Who wouldn't want you for these parts? You are the Bullock's underwear man, for crying out loud!"

He propped his elbows on the rail at the park's edge above the waves. "You just don't understand, Faith."

But I did. Living on the verge gave Tag nothing to grab hold of. When he felt desirable by those in his profession, the world was a wonderful place. But if his photo or audition was brushed off, all was despair. He simply could not handle life when he wasn't the most dazzling one out of a pool of virtually thousands.

As for me, I had a choice to make. Join him on the verge, ignore his selfishness, and do my best to help him battle his insecurities, or go nose to nose with the rattlesnakes. I decided to keep trying, and together, our days and nights ebbed and flowed like the tide that slammed itself against the sand down the street.

Eventually, Tag stopped coming home some nights, and one dark early morning, I flipped on the light when he stumbled in drunk.

"Where've you been?"

He ignored my question.

"Tag," I tried again. "Where were you?"

He looked at me like I was crazy and stuck his finger in my face. "I don't have to answer to you."

"Hey, I have the right to know where you've been."

"Shut up, Faith." Tag dropped onto the sofa and pulled a joint out of his pocket. "Doesn't this piss you off, huh, Miss Goodie Two-shoes?" He struck a match and drew in a deep drag.

I just stared.

"Come on, Faith," Tag rose and came over to me. "Doesn't this make you want to have a conniption fit?" He took another long hit and blew the smoke in my face.

I didn't respond.

Tag flopped down on the couch, grabbed the television remote, and started clicking through the channels. Within minutes, he was passed out cold.

Just then, the phone rang.

Marcy. Again. Marcy. Always. "Let me talk to Tag!" she shrilled.

"Here you go, Tag!" my voice snapped as I tossed the phone.

But he must have been half-asleep. Or really high. Definitely slow on the uptake.

The receiver flew across the coffee table and smacked him in the face.

"Nice going, Faith." Tag gasped as he began bleeding from a nostril. "I think you just ruined my career."

I grabbed tissues and tried to wipe his blood. "Oh, Tag, I'm so sorry."

"An actor's face is really all he's got." Tag scowled at me.

So, as fate would have it, one of Tag's first big breaks in Hollywood was the main bone running widthwise on his nose.

"The nasal bone," a doctor confirmed, looking over his glasses at us in the examination room.

Tag never saw it coming.

But neither did I. Not back on my daddy's porch, or at Bustiani's wine party, or the day I chose the circus over the solid ground beneath my feet.

The third thing to go was the romance.

Let's face it. When you're shacking up with a narcissistic egomaniac, a bunch of cockroaches, and the threat of rattlesnakes, the last thing you want to do is drop your guard, close your eyes, and pretend you mean it when you wrap your arms around some guy you gave up on a long time ago.

Besides, the only thing Tag loved as much as himself anymore was the television set.

"Are you kidding me?" he yelled at a Sprite commercial while camped out on the couch across from the TV screen. "I was up for that ad! They picked that creep?"

The distance between us had grown so humongous I might as well have been vacuuming lint balls off the ugliest carpeting on Mars, instead of standing on it just a few feet from Tag in our little circus apartment on the parade route.

"Wait! I gotta see this!" he snapped, sliding both me and the vacuum to the side after I accidentally blocked his view.

Another time, I was swishing the feather duster around the place, and he demanded I move so he could get a better look at *Cheers*.

"Do you mind, Faith?" Tag sounded exasperated. "I'm trying to study my craft here."

I turned away from him.

What on earth was I still doing here? In this place? With this circus performer?

I wasn't vacuuming or dusting or waitressing up the street or living near the ocean anymore. I was dying inside. With riveting focus, I zeroed in on the Holy Bible that sat on my bookshelf across the room. That was it. My absolute redemption. My utter salvation. My only way out. Out of LA. The perpetual gloom of this place. My current life circumstances. Away from Tag's moods, the rotten, horrible life I'd chosen with him, and all the hate that boiled inside me.

I dropped the duster, walked to the bookshelf, pulled that Bible out, split it up the middle, and began to read. Through tears I softly cried with the psalmist, "The Lord is my rock, my fortress and my deliverer."

The music wailed as Tag's show ended and the closing credits rolled.

I half expected "That's a wrap!" as he got off the couch. Then he showered and put on his complimentary Bullock's underwear and clothes. He opened the fridge, popped the top on a beer, and sat back down to worship his god of choice, the almighty television set, with his trigger hand firing up the remote.

From the other side of the room, I looked past him to watch the breeze scrape a palm frond across the window glass.

Tag let out a heavy sigh. Not once did he stop watching *Miami Vice* to look at my face.

The next thing to go was my Bible.

One day, it was simply gone. After I looked for it for hours, I finally concluded that Tag must have gotten drunk and taken it, to hide it from me, or toss it out.

"Tag, please," I begged him. "That Bible has such sentimental value, from way back when I was a little girl. Signed by Pastor Watkins, and by Mama and Daddy. With all my healing scriptures underlined."

"You and your stupid Bible, Faith." Tag combed his fingers through his hair. All of his knuckle warts were back on both hands now. But he was getting steady acting jobs in spite of them. And the crooked nasal bone.

"You *soooo* needed a flaw, sweetheart," Marcy Steiner had gushed to Tag soon after the telephone cracked his nose. "You were entirely too perfect. The phones will be ringing off the hook for you now, honey."

But where was my Bible?

As soon as Tag left for the day, I headed outside, where any observer of the 12th Street parade might have described my actions as dumpster diving. But I knew good and well from the homeless and the humiliated, this kind of thing was serious business. With yet another overcast sky weighing down on me, I went hunting in the alley behind 12th Street, knee-high in fresh garbage, dumpster to dumpster, on a desperate search for my Bible.

Minutes later, a low voice startled me from behind. "What do you need, miss?" It was Quarters. With both arms stretched out, he offered me everything he had. Coins in one hand, a half-eaten donut in the other.

"Oh, Quarters." I fought back my tears. "I'm looking for the most valuable thing I own. My Bible, with my name handwritten inside. All my personal information about my home and my church and my baptism and Sunday school, too. I don't think I can live without it."

Quarters nodded solemnly. Living without. It was a topic he understood all too well.

One shimmering afternoon, as silver light dropped all the way down Montana Avenue, I watched Tag for several minutes from a storefront window. Some redhead with a knockout figure and a model's portfolio case was planting kisses down his neck over cocktails at the Patio Café across the street. She laughed. He laughed. They kissed.

When he finally came home that next night, I told him I was leaving, and with dramatic Hollywood flair the curtain toppled down onto the bitter end of us.

Tag lashed out at me, shaking his rattles and baring his venomous fangs. He grabbed my shoulder. Hard. This boy I'd known forever. The cutest guy from Modesto. The one who looked like a movie star. The *Playgirl* model who couldn't keep his jeans buttoned. The Bullock's underwear man.

He let go.

He walked to the fridge, opened a can of beer, and headed out the front door. His footsteps quickly merged onto the parade route to join the rest of the procession outside.

Moments later, I ran into the living room with my suitcase packed, ransacking the place for my car keys. I finally found them at the bottom of my purse. My head throbbed as my heart pounded in my chest.

When a muffled noise sounded at the door, I froze, certain that Tag was back. But the peephole revealed nothing but sandy dreadlocks. I flung open the door to find Quarters, standing very still and silent. He held out my Bible as I burst into tears.

I was still crying when I stuffed two backpacks full of Tag's shoes, T-shirts, jeans, and enough still-in-the-package Bullock's underwear to last the rest of Quarters's years. Then we hit the jackpot when I scrounged Tag's pockets for spare change, and found four hundred dollars instead.

"I'll never forget you, Quarters." I handed him the backpacks and the money.

"I won't forget you either, Faith Countryman." It was the first time he'd ever called me by name. "Or the Bible you couldn't live without."

I threw my arms around Quarters's bony shoulders and matted hair. Gently, he hugged me back, and the sour scent of too many nights on the streets pressed its weary perfume between us.

The last thing to go was the television remote control device.

On my way out of LA, as I turned my back on apartment 10, the circus, the parade, the fog, the roaches, and the rattlesnakes, I swung open the kitchen window and chucked that thing over two fences. A dog howled as it hit the cement and shattered to bits.

~

With a stomp on the gas, I raced like mad to escape from the worst years of my life. Rounding the corner of Wilshire, I watched the nighttime sky uncork, as rain began to pour. Within minutes, water was everywhere, streaming from awnings to walkways, and funneling from tires as I sped for the freeway.

Something about this storm was oddly familiar. It crashed down heavy and hard, as if like the one from my birth. When the crops flooded, the animals drowned, and the men lost their profits and their minds. When Mama screamed her lungs out, trying to work me free from her body.

Free. Free. I was free now.

I whipped into the fast lane and shot out of sight from the headlights behind.

I was hightailing it. Like the jackrabbits back on Rumble Road.

"Get 'em, Dad!" My brothers had jumped up from the dinner table to see our daddy bolt out the door again, to chase those jacks out of our vegetable garden.

"There they go." The boys watched through a window.

"All the way to the walnut tree."

"They . . . got . . . away." Daddy finally returned, panting, slapping dust off his legs. "Little varmints."

How I loved those dinners. When my usually quiet and subdued daddy acted like a crazy kook, then grinned and winked across the table at me afterward.

"If you're ever running for your life," Daddy advised, "or just dead set on getting somewhere quick, you'd better hightail it like one of those rabbits!"

So, I pressed on along the dark freeway. Never stopping. Not even once. In the middle of all that blazing remorse and cascading rain.

MODESTO,
CALIFORNIA

~

It was early morning when I made the turn back to the ranch where I was born. To drive under skies integrated with bold color. Periwinkles on gold. Lilacs streaked through amber. The ground was wet and the air was chilly, but I rolled down my windows anyway to get my fill of this place.

When I was a kid, Rumble Road seemed stretched both wide and long, but now it was shrunken smaller than any of my recollections. New paint brightened the house. The chimney chain-smoked billows out its brick casing. John Deeres lined up behind the shed. The barn door hung closed, but still crooked, in the most charming of dilapidated ways.

I slowed on the driveway to watch a big yellow dog I'd never seen before wake up on the front step. He raised his head and stared through my windshield. From deep in the porch shadows, my daddy stood to lean over the rail with his shoulders sloped more than before. Then his eyes squinted, lifting at the corners as he smiled as big as ever. Like he'd just chased a jackrabbit all the way to the walnut tree and winked and grinned at me afterward.

Daddy couldn't even get near me, though, 'cause the door flew wide open, and Mama leaped off the porch in the loudest lime-green sweat suit you ever saw, shrieking and scaring the daylights out of the dog. With her hands on her cheeks, the tears poured out of her. Living proof of a love so wild and strong, she could almost forget the night I broke her heart.

They didn't exactly kill the fatted calf that night, but Mama roasted wild game hens from Paulson's Poultry & Egg Ranch, inviting my brothers and their newly budding families for supper. We drank our coffee long afterward, looking out at the peach trees. At Daddy's withered brown harem ladies, frozen dormant in the vineyard. At a big pregnant moon, slung low, glowing off the darkness.

There was nothing but forgiveness that night. The prodigal daughter had come home. I'd fought the forces of Hell to get there, too. Longing, aching, for this moment to wash over us, to put the Kingdom Come back inside of me again.

～

Call me slow as molasses in a snowstorm, because it took another seven years before I finally went to the place I was destined for. But it just so happened that seven was the big number of perfection and completion, biblically speaking. Seven days of creation. Seven marches around the wall of Jericho. Seven dips in the Jordan River. Seven years of Tribulation. If anyone ever asked God to pick a number between one and ten, take my word. Seven. Every time.

As horrible and gloomy as Santa Monica was on some of those scary days back at the circus on the 12th Street parade route, being in my childhood bedroom had a little dark gloom cloud all its own. With each month that passed, I knew that something was absolutely wrong here. I'd worn out my welcome and should've been gone by now. But where? And doing what?

My future seemed blurred with confusion as I became more desperate to get on with it. What *it* was, I had no idea.

Mama, bless her heart, did her best to restrain herself from all the I-told-you-so's she could have hurled in my direction. But don't think she didn't have her ways of getting her points across.

"Follow a skunk, and he'll stink up your life," she blurted out one day over breakfast.

"Hmmm."

Another morning while we weeded the garden, it was, "Don't ever give your hog the day's best food."

"Hmmm."

By the time she spouted, "Fools and chickens are full of the dickens," I just had to set her straight.

"Mama"—I propped myself against the handle of the backhoe—"I promise I'll never go and do anything like that again."

But Mama could talk out both sides of her mouth. And go ahead and call her starstruck while you're at it, 'cause when Tag Barone suddenly appeared on TV, in living color, in a McDonald's commercial, grinning ridiculously, almost seductively, at a quarter-pounder with cheese, she went absolutely bonkers.

"There he is! Faith, it's Tag! It's him!" From all her commotion, you'd have thought that Frank Sinatra, Tom Jones, and Robert Redford had just marched into our living room to put on a talent show.

"That's him all right, Mama."

She gasped. "What on God's green earth happened to that boy's nose?"

～

No doubt, Mama would have added her two cents about idle hands being the devil's playground. But before I gave her any chance of that, I turned myself into the woman most likely to be lacking idle hands. I attended college courses until I received my degree. I helped with the daily chores inside and out. I began walking several miles each day for exercise with Daddy's big yellow dog, Solomon. I practiced the piano by ear until hundreds of harmonized melodies were banked in my memory's musical repertoire. I worked part-time in the office of the First Baptist Church, typing, filing, and answering phones. I taught Sunday school to kindergartners, and color-crayoned so many pictures of Jesus that one day our Lord and Savior ended up with Indian turquoise eyes and fire-red hair, dressed in a kelly-green robe ensemble with sparkly silver sandals.

"Who's that guy?" a serious little boy inquired beside me.

I wadded up the drawing and slam-dunked it in the garbage can. Trash-can basketball. Add that to the list of things I suddenly excelled at while trying not to be idle.

On the search to jazz things up, make my life more meaningful, and to perhaps find some direction in the meantime, I began visiting Meadows Hospital once a week. To hold hands with the sick, and the scared, and the dying. To watch with my own eyes all of those who became well. Some gradually, others overnight, and for a few, instantaneously. It was impossible not to notice that so many sickly souls became healthy again. Power of God, miraculous signs and wonders, church-verified spiritual gift of healing aside, I had to wonder if sometimes folks were just destined to go on living rather than dying.

You didn't have to be a genius to figure out that something was missing from my life. I was triple-spinning my wheels, but going absolutely nowhere, frozen in place and time. I just didn't know what to do with myself.

Until the day Mr. Rexford Swanson knocked on our door.

Seven times.

～

I was expecting it to be one of Mama's emaciated hobos. One of those dusty train hoppers, who occasionally appeared on our side lawn, sniffing around for Mama's roast beef sandwiches. But this time the knock was coming from the front door. Tapping right off the smooth knuckles of a portly man in a real nice suit with a Mercedes Benz parked behind him. His shoes and briefcase looked like spit-shined crocodile or alligator, garden lizard, for all I knew. Whatever the case, this guy stuck out like a sore thumb out here off Rumble Road.

"Good afternoon." He handed me his business card when I opened the screen. "I'm Rexford Swanson, here on official legal business, and I'm looking for a Miss Faith Countryman."

"I'm Faith Countryman, sir."

We shook hands, and he gestured to the porch chairs. "May we sit down, Miss Countryman? I have some important documents to show you."

"To show *me*? Really?" I scanned the vineyard for my daddy, but Lord knows, he wouldn't have known what to do with this spiffy-dressed half reptile of a man either.

"This matter involves Mr. David Doone. Do you remember him?"

"David Doone," I repeated the name softly. "No, sorry, I've never known anyone by that name."

Mr. Swanson placed a manila file folder in my hands. "There's a letter for you on top." His demeanor grew solemn. "It's blunt and to the point. You might need to prepare yourself first, Miss Countryman."

Not knowing David Doone, I wondered what kind of preparing I could possibly do. I took the sheet of paper and began to read:

Dear Faith Countryman:

If you're reading this, I'm dead and gone. But I guess I wasn't really living for a long time anyway.

I want you to know that I had a big life once. I had a wife, and a home, too, a beautiful place in Northern California. Then one day my wife was hit by a car and killed, and nothing was ever the same. I couldn't stay in our house after she was gone, but I didn't have the heart to sell it either. So I just walked down the street and out of town. Forever.

With your kindness still fresh in my mind, I'm giving you my old house in Cross Creek, California. It's been kept up all these years by neighbors across the street, so it should be ready for moving in, if that's what you decide to do.

Some say there are no mistakes in life. Maybe that's why we found each other. Both of us, lost. Like your Bible that night. Lost in the fog. In a place neither one of us could really call home.

Good luck in Cross Creek.

Your friend, Quarters

The letter was also signed "David Doone" and witnessed by the man on my front porch.

"Quarters? He had a house?"

"He gave up on everything when his wife died. Before that, he was quite a different man."

"Modesto is a long way from 12th Street in Santa Monica, sir. How did you find me?"

"Mr. Doone said he copied your personal information from the inside cover of your Bible one night."

I smiled, and passed the folder back to him. "Thank you, Mr. Swanson. It was nice of you to come all this way, but I can't accept such a gift. I barely knew him."

"Well, you must have made quite an impression." He handed the folder back to me, along with the property's title and deed, and a ballpoint pen.

"No way. This is crazy."

"Miss Countryman, I remember the day he came into my office to put your name on these documents. He was wearing brand-new shoes. He said they were a gift from an angel." Mr. Swanson smiled. "He really wanted to give you this house."

Sunlight edged up the porch and onto his crackly briefcase as he sat, waiting patiently, wiping his brow with his handkerchief, his clean fingernails tapping the file folder.

"Didn't he have anyone else? Some friend or a relative?"

"Not a soul." Mr. Swanson placed another file in my hand. "Take it, Miss Countryman." He smacked the big crocodile mouth of his briefcase shut. "You can do whatever you want with the house. Keep it, sell it, give it to charity, live there the rest of your life. It's your decision, but, please, accept this token from this man." He looked me straight in the eye. "He didn't have a lot of wishes left in this world. This, however, was one of them."

Rexford Swanson's crocodile shoes slid back into his sleek Mercedes.

I looked down at the folder in my lap. Neatly typed on the label was my name with the address of a house in Cross Creek, a place I'd never been or ever even heard of.

I watched Rexford Swanson's Mercedes roll down Rumble Road, where it passed a truck carrying its load. Hay. Beautiful tawny-gold bales, dried and bundled. Cubes of free wishes stacked taller than the cab.

He didn't have a lot of wishes left in this world. This, however, was one of them.

So, there it was. Clear as day.

I was about to get on with it. Finally. In a place I knew nothing about, except that an old friend had been healthy and whole there. That his house sat waiting for me. And that the very thought of going had already caused my gloom to vanish and lifted my spirits sky high.

CROSS CREEK,
CALIFORNIA

~

I found Cross Creek late in the morning, nestled against crooks in a hillside and wrapped in a cocoon of yesteryears. It was the kind of place where light bathed luminous. Where redwood storefronts lined avenues that meandered and intersected at quiet junctions and shady corners. No matter which way you turned, the creek rushed by, beside or beneath you, and bridges provided footpaths and just enough room for two cars at once.

Beyond the town's center, residential streets crawled under trees with branches linked beneath blue skies. Farther up were emerald hills that spread checkered fields with ranches and school houses. Elevated on the highest ridges were church steeples, their spires taller than the treetops.

Solomon stretched his head out the window as far as he could reach. I gave him a pat, then turned to circle Main Street again.

Daddy had been sad but insistent about me bringing his sweet dog here.

"Oh, I'll miss him all right," he said, scratching Solomon's chin and handing me his leash and brush. "But he'll keep you safe in that town you know nothing about. He'll keep you company, too."

"I'll have him back before you know it," I reassured Daddy as we loaded my boxes that morning. "I'm staying in Cross Creek just long enough to sell Mr. Doone's house."

Daddy nodded and waved goodbye as I pressed the gas. All the while, Solomon calmly sat in the passenger seat like a human waiting to go on a road trip.

"Morning, miss," the driver of an oncoming car called out as he passed.

"Oh! Morning!"

Cars were parked on Main Street where hitching posts used to be, beside shops with wooden stairs and overhang porches. A few men with coffee cups and Cokes in bottles sat in chairs, along with some authentic-looking cowboys in boots, hats, and even chaps. I hadn't seen that attire for years, and you couldn't really count the boys back on Santa Monica Boulevard in LA, because they wore eyeliner, too.

I drove past a group of women on a bench who stopped their conversation midsentence to stare. When I waved, they nearly tore their armpits loose waving back at me.

"Solomon, people might be gathered for chitchat, but I got a hunch that homes don't sell like hotcakes around here." I took a deep breath. "We'll need professional help."

Scanning storefronts for a real estate office, I found everything else instead. A one-room city hall with an attached courthouse, a library, and a sheriff's department next to the bank. The Coffee Pot Cafe, and the Tree House Restaurant. A bakery, the Mill Grocery and Grain Store, a bookstore, and an antique/gift shop. I noticed a music studio with "Guitar Lessons" handwritten on a chalkboard in the window. The beer hall on the corner was called the Monkey Bar. An old cottage had been remodeled into a law firm/insurance office. Critters Animal Hospital stood next to the Creekside Medical Center, next door to Smiley's Dental Office.

"I think that's it," I told Solomon. "Now, let's go find our house."

It wasn't hard to run into Smith Street. Four blocks higher than town, it rose on a gradual slope, with lawns sprawled like shimmering blankets, maples canopied overhead, and American flags fluttering off front-porch pillars.

The house was all the way up the street on the left. Past ranch-style and Craftsman homes, the colorful gardens, a man washing his car, a woman pulling weeds, and a dog who peeped an eye open at a kid on a skateboard. Holy moly! I'd just driven straight into the American Dream only to top it off by parking in front of the most adorable house on the block. A two-story white-on-white Victorian with gingerbread trim and a big ebony door.

"Hang on to your fur balls, Solomon." I jerked the brake into position and climbed out of the truck. "Who on earth *wouldn't* want to buy this place? It's amazing."

I couldn't believe my eyes. Or that Quarters had ever deserted this place, leaving it empty for so long. His letter mentioned that the neighbors across the street had been tending to the property. But that hardly summed it up. This was one immaculate little estate dripping with charm and ultimate curb appeal. Its paint was fresh. The yard was healthy and green with a huge oak and meticulously trimmed walkways and brick seams. The planters were full of hundreds of blooming flowers.

I walked along the sidewalk as Solomon sniffed, exploring the yard. Up the driveway to a stone path, we found a little detached garage and a backyard that extended out to a hill north of the property. Bushes of bright-pink and peach roses dangled over a small pond where a fountain trickled under a statue of a young woman with a perpetual marbleized grin.

Even the hammock strung between two birches looked to be in good, if not new, condition. I flopped into its sling of canvas, laughing at my unexpected good fortune just as a pair of voices called out from the front yard.

"Hello?"

"Anybody back here?"

Solomon barked, then growled as I wrestled and swung my way out of the hammock.

Two young men suddenly appeared on the path.

"Hi, I'm Marc Merriweather," said one. "This is my brother, Brett. We live across the street."

"Are you the ones who've been taking such good care of this place?"

"Well, yeah, I guess you could say so."

"Our parents did all the work here for years."

"But we took over when our dad died," chimed in his brother. "And since our mom's fingers got messed up with arthritis."

"Well, thank you for all your time and trouble." I shook hands with them.

"We thought you might need a welcome to the neighborhood." Marc smiled.

"And a hand unpacking your truck." Brett grabbed a box out of the truck bed and headed up the porch.

"Thanks." I led the way with the key, then twisted the brass knob on the big black door. It swung wide open on its hinges, and I gasped.

"It's quite a place, isn't it?" one of them softly asked.

All I could manage was a nod as I stepped across the threshold.

They carefully set the boxes in the hallway, where a stream of sunlight speckled the smooth walnut floorboards.

I turned to them, astonished. "I'm Faith, by the way. Faith Countryman."

TESTIMONY
LUCINDA MERRIWEATHER

~

*W*hen *Faith Countryman came to town, I had the bird's-eye view. My house was directly across from Doone's old place, and our front doors faced one another like two sentries posted at the top of Smith Street. Not that I liked to snoop, but this being the first activity in decades at the place, I was more than curious.*

What a day it was. Fresh morning warmth. Light shimmering every-where. I heard her the second she arrived and rooted the brake on her truck, then watched as a big gold dog tumbled out behind her. Together, they walked along the sidewalk, and studied the surrounding homes. With a pat on the dog's head, she shifted her gaze toward my house, and I had to be quick to duck behind my lace curtains in time.

My two sons were home that summer. In their early twenties, full of hamburgers, hot rods, and hormones. All the girls in town were crazy about them. Brett had the washboard stomach. Marc had the smile. And both boys nearly killed themselves getting out the door and across the street to help our new neighbor with her bags and boxes and trunks. Never mind the to-do list I'd Scotch-taped on the refrigerator door three weeks prior. They were dying to lift and tote Faith Countryman's belongings into that Victorian. At one point, Brett pulled off his T-shirt and stuffed it into his back pocket. Marc displayed his pearly whites with one continuous grin.

I quickly discovered that my new neighbor was not only attractive, but brimming over with personality. Her sort of charisma was hard to come by anymore, especially in a world full of losers, lunatics, and downright spoiled brats. Even from across the street, I could tell that hers was the kind of charm I'd never possessed. Not even on my best days. Not when I met my beloved Roger, or walked down the aisle in my wedding gown, or in those so-called glowing months of pregnancy, which was just a nice way of saying fat, sweaty, and spreading out thick in the belly, and in my case, across the bridge of the nose. The fact that Marc and Brett were such lookers was one of those freak accidents that occurs when two very plain people conceive and happen to hit the gene-pool lottery. Little miracles, really.

Little did I know that miracles were about to become regular topics of conversation in Cross Creek that summer.

I peered out from behind the drapes again. How much time does it take to drop a suitcase on the floor and be on your merry way?

I couldn't hear their exact words, but no one could miss the sound of exuberant conversation mixed with boisterous laughter. All of it shot through the Victorian's entry hall and out the open door.

"What on earth could be so hilarious?" I demanded aloud as I glared out the window.

Suddenly, the most intense fear began to grip me with its ugly claw. Was it possible this woman was dreadfully wrong for this place, this town, and our little Smith Street? Could she have been the corrupt city type who'd come to Cross Creek to perpetrate some scam? Or to prey on all the men, including the sons of aging, forgotten widows? And to what depths had she stooped to force a lonely man like David Doone to name her as the sole beneficiary of his property?

*At dinner over cold ham sandwiches, Brett went on and on about her.
"That Faith Countryman." He sighed. "She's really something."*

"Sure is," Marc added with a nod.

I nearly choked on a mouthful of secret-family-recipe potato salad.

*"That's quite enough about our new neighbor," I said firmly. "She's
much older than you boys. Why, she could almost be your mother." I sniffed.
Really, though, she wasn't that old, decades younger than me. But I'd given
birth very late in life, in my midforties.*

"A young aunt, perhaps," Brett suggested.

"A slightly older cousin," Marc corrected.

My boys exchanged a look that made me very uncomfortable.

*Right after supper, Faith Countryman started all that racket on her
piano.*

*"Oh great," I muttered from the parlor as soon as the first notes floated
across the street. "We got Liberace in the neighborhood now."*

*My arthritic fingers stitched my needlepoint as the melodies slowly
became recognizable. Listening closely, I heard our new neighbor's voice lift
like a songbird, rising to fill the warm night with an ambiance we'd never
quite experienced on Smith Street. Were those hymns? I was astounded. "I
Surrender All," "When the Roll Is Called Up Yonder," "The Old Rugged
Cross," "Blessed Assurance." These were songs I'd adored my entire life.*

*"Imagine that." I paused, then stabbed my needle through the hoop.
Shaking out my crooked fingers, the pain crackled through my joints and
caused me to wince. Carefully, I felt the stitches. Flat and taut, still perfect,
despite the condition of my poor eyesight and wretched fingers.*

*As my new neighbor's clear notes continued to levitate on air, I couldn't
resist joining in, "Oh, what a foretaste of glory divine."*

*For the first time since Faith Countryman's arrival that morning, my
heart steadied to its deepest calm. Truly, I hadn't felt such inner peace in a
very long while.*

*By the time I was ready to turn in for bed, Faith Countryman had
played enough hymns for an entire church service. She ended her repertoire*

by belting out a hard and husky rendition of "Steamed Heat," sounding like a blues queen in a smoky bar, bent over a microphone and giving a bunch of sailors something to remember.

My smile gave way to a chuckle. I got up and flipped down the light switch. With a finger snap that normally would have caused my digits to ache for days, I sashayed my hips from side to side all the way down the hall to my bedroom. Feeling no pain, I settled my head on the pillow and fell fast asleep.

~

Cradled by the fluffiest sheets and pillowcases imaginable, I was beyond rested when morning's glow bled into the day. I barely heard the soft thud of the newspaper as it dropped anchor on the neighbor's porch. Or the swoosh of the sprinkler's arm, weeping across the Merriweathers' lawn. Finally, I squinted at the impatiens in the window box, at the minty-green walls that surrounded me in the master suite.

"Morning, Solomon," I whispered, stepping around his legs stretched out on the floor beside me.

Had I died and gone to Heaven? Seriously! Was it possible I'd dreamt up this whole place?

I padded down the hallway from one room to the next. People didn't really inherit beautiful homes from folks they barely knew, did they?

In the parlor, I stepped from smoothly polished planks onto a handwoven rug, then curled up into the heavy fabric of a tapestry-woven settee. In the dining room, I brushed my fingertip the length of the long dining table. I pressed a perfectly tuned middle C on the black baby grand in the music room where I'd played the night before.

"Okay, Solomon," I said as I dropped into a wicker chair under the heat of the glass-domed sunroom. "We're not dreaming after all. This place is the real deal."

I unpacked in record time, all of my things delegated to the drawers in the oak highboy dresser and the cedar-lined wardrobe. I'd brought only summer clothes to Cross Creek, figuring I'd sell the house and get back home before the weather cooled. Now, after seeing how small and out of the way this place was, I wasn't so sure. Unless some Cross Creek resident had been eyeing the Victorian all these years, a quick sale seemed like a long shot.

I flopped onto the master bed and sank into the soft down of the comforter. "Solomon, what would be so utterly absurd about us deciding to keep this place? As a vacation home, maybe?"

He cocked his golden head at me.

"I know. I know. We're the furthest things from the vacation home types."

Within minutes, I was submerged in bubbles in the ball-and-claw tub in the master bath while Solomon sat patiently on the corner of the needlepoint runner in the dressing room.

"We'd be smart to think twice about that vacation home idea, Solomon," I called out over the edge of the tub to him.

Solomon flopped down on his belly.

With one more splatter, I dunked all the way under, then grabbed a towel.

～

Wavy heat rippled off a late afternoon sun as I followed the roads back to Main Street. I parked in front of the Mill Grocery and Grain Supply, a building made entirely out of logs.

"Stay right here, boy." I scratched Solomon's head and left him in the truck bed.

"Welcome to Cross Creek, ma'am." The voice could have belonged to any one of several men drinking coffee and Cokes underneath the overhang roof of the porch.

"Thanks."

The Mill wasn't your everyday grocery store. It was dark inside, and backed up on a real shocker of a view that looked out over a wide expanse of the creek. There was an old mill and a water wheel next to willows and mossy banks, with canoes drifting by. The market was also unique, because it equally catered to both humans and animals. One entire room was stocked with hay, alfalfa, grain, and equipment for livestock, while the other had all the items for human consumption.

After picking out Solomon's food, I headed to the produce bins, filled with fruits and vegetables, nuts and beans. Then I pushed my cart to the butcher counter for chicken and fish fillets.

Rounding the next aisle, I came face-to-face with a man so ridiculously handsome, it would have been impossible to prepare myself for the sight of him. He was tall and lean, but muscular, with brown hair and a perfectly chiseled face. He wore beat-up jeans and a T-shirt that tugged against his broad shoulders. And he was completely unfazed. Either oblivious to my stupefied reaction, or so accustomed to this sort of thing that it didn't ruffle him one bit.

Quickly steering his cart, he allowed me by. But for the second that his eyes met mine, my stomach flipped.

I looked away as he headed for the register.

Holy smokes! How would it feel to have a guy like that bringing home the groceries?

By the time I was back outside loading bags in my truck, a big pile of loneliness had landed on top of me. I figured that was to be expected in a new town all by myself. It would have been different if I was in love in a place like this. In love with some wonderful man.

I sighed and patted Solomon's head.

But that's when everything changed. All because Solomon started barking his head off at a pitiful-looking soul who looked like death warmed over as he shuffled along the sidewalk next to us.

Mustering the strength to climb the stairs, the man was skin and bones, ghostly pale, chemo-bald with no eyelashes, eyebrows, or a single hair follicle anywhere. Somehow, he'd ended up right here in front of me, with one foot in the grave and the other on the Mill's bottom step.

I offered up a little silent prayer on his behalf and reached for the door handle. Then I froze, knowing perfectly well that such a carelessly offered, random prayer would never be up to snuff, especially for a practicing Baptist with the church-verified spiritual gift of healing. Full of chills now, I turned back to him—to let go, to allow myself to be drawn, impossibly and desperately, to this corpse of a man.

"Excuse me, sir." I stepped behind him as he held onto the Mill's handrail for dear life. "Can I help you?"

"I doubt it." He kept his back turned.

I followed him up the step anyway. "What's your name?"

He glanced at me skeptically. "Why?"

"Please, just give me your name."

"It's Stan." He blinked. "Stan Jackson."

"Hi, Stan. I'm new to Cross Creek."

"No kidding."

"I just moved into David Doone's old Victorian up Smith Street." I reached for his hand. "Please, just hang on to me real tight for a minute."

The hairless mounds above his eyes arched as he gave me both of his bony, dried-out hands.

"Stan Jackson." I caressed his fingers. "What are you doing tonight?"

"Dying. What are you doing?"

I dropped his hands as my voice rose in anger. "Shut your face!"

Stan Jackson looked absolutely slap-shocked. He glanced around, like he hoped someone would come rescue him from scary ol' me. But there was no one in sight, and all the men on the porch were long gone.

"Lady, I don't know what you're trying to do here, but . . ."

"Listen to me. You will not survive your disease while spouting words of sickness and death. That's called negative confession! That'll kill ya!"

"No offense, but I'm dying already. And I'm really tired right now. I just want to go inside, get my Jose Cuervo and my Twinkies. Then I'm gonna go home, watch TV, and wait around till I die."

"Don't you dare talk like that!"

"Well, look at me! I'm in the final stages here. What idiot in my position would have a cheery outlook?"

"Shhh!" I grabbed his shoulders, feeling his collarbones poking straight through. "Stan Jackson, I'm telling you right now, you'd better speak life from this point on. Speak life and live, or speak death and die. It's that simple."

"Oh yeah? That simple, huh?"

"You're gonna get exactly what you say. You say it. You get it. Manifestations from the spiritual world swooping right down into the natural realm. Just like that."

"Lady . . ."

"Listen to me, Stan Jackson. I'm coming over tonight. We're gonna get you reborn. Anointed with oil, baptized by the Holy Spirit. There's no time to waste. We'll use prayer cloths, the laying on of hands, the slaying of the spirit, Communion, speaking in tongues, whatever it takes."

He shook his head. "Lady, I think you probably mean well, but no one can help me now. I'm way past that."

I jerked on his scrawny arm so hard, he nearly lost his balance. "My name isn't Lady. It's Faith, and they didn't give me that name for nothing. Like it or not, I'm coming over later to save your life."

He sighed. "Oh, whatever!" Trembling, he finally reached the top step and turned. "I know the house you're talking about. I'll send my buddy Race McGee over to pick you up. By the way, he didn't get that name for nothing either, so fasten your seat belt."

"Fasten yours, baby."

TESTIMONY

STAN JACKSON

~

*P*icture something you hated losing. A bet, a game, a girl, a day fallen
    to waste, anything that sank your heart to the floor. For me, it was
standing at a bitter edge and surrendering all my hopes. It was the last glow
of afternoon light. It was a beautiful woman dropping my hand and turning away. These were my losses one summer when all the time in the world
had whittled down to nothing.

I was exhausted when she finally got to me, every ounce of energy spent
on the effort of visualizing things I wouldn't see or do again, along with
others I'd never really considered. Suddenly, the fact I'd never tried skydiving
had me itching to jump out of a plane.

"I won't see the jungles of Costa Rica now," I said. As if I'd ever given
a rip. "No chance of becoming a father." A tear began to roll. "There's just
not enough time."

Earlier that morning, the doctors had told me, "It's all touch and go
from here." They delivered my prognosis evening-broadcast style, their iced

voices cutting swiftly, their eyes blank and blameless, rejecting liability for things gone wrong.

I was altogether enraged and horrified as the doctors watched my reaction, then looked away to scribble illegible handwriting on my chart. "Whatcha writing there, huh?" I demanded. "'Dead as a doornail'?"

That evening, the heat raged as the last of an orange sunset splashed down in the west. After months of looking at a whole bunch of nothing, or at my bony face with the crap scared out of it in the mirror, it was how I suddenly saw everything that snapped my head around. The light as it poured across the sky. A team of clouds tearing apart in silvery strands. A breeze from nowhere softly pushing against the house. A bottle of tequila on the kitchen countertop, shimmering like liquid gold.

Finally, in the middle of it all, Faith Countryman arrived, happy as a clam, ready to jack me up and save the world.

The tumors were running rampant by then, but I managed to stand up when she arrived and climbed out of Race McGee's Chevy into a gulf of dry heat. All the way to the curb, she stared at the cornstalks next to my driveway. It was a pathetic crop, parched and perishing in the very season it was meant to flourish. But I'd given up on that corn a while back. Along with everything else.

Faith followed Race up the driveway. When her eyes met mine through the window, she tilted her chin to acknowledge me, and I had to grab hold of the sink for balance. It almost felt like my heart was beating stronger, or my motor was running faster, but for all I knew, another malignant tumor was bouncing around inside me.

As soon as she stepped into my kitchen, I got a good whiff of her fragrance. She smelled fresh and fruity, like a truckload of raspberries with a twist of lime.

"Hey, Stan." Her voice sounded almost melodious. She walked straight over to me, the heels of her sandals making a tremendous racket across my floor. She took hold of my forearm and a smile broke across her face. "You ready?"

I nodded.

Her fingers squeezed. "You're still breathing, aren't you?"

I nodded again, deliberately exhaling.

"Whatever you do"—she paused for effect—"don't forget to breathe." With surprising strength, she pulled me close. "And while you're at it, don't forget to live." She backed up a step and parked her hands on her hips. "That's the point of all this." Her eyes closed for a few seconds. "That's why we're all here, loving you like crazy."

All? The only other person around was Race, and he was about as far as a guy could get from loving me like crazy. He half rolled his eyes and stood beside my stack of dirty dishes, not having a clue what to do next. Finally, he just pulled the shot glasses off the shelf and started pouring. I sank into one of my vinyl kitchen chairs, trying to focus, while tears burned at the rims of my eyes.

Faith Countryman started to pace across my kitchen floor. "Okay, this is it, Stan!" she exclaimed as her heels made their way across my linoleum.

I found myself suddenly noticing that my kitchen floor was filthy. Come to think of it, the whole house was a mess. Already, clumps of dirt clung to her heels.

But all that pacing of hers sounded so solid, like a heart beating or a clock ticking. Maybe this noise could march into my subconscious, keep time until the end, then finally let me go sliding away. I could blast through that long tunnel everyone's always coming back from the other side to talk about. Shoot like a rocket for that bright light at the end. The end was coming. I was about as dead as all that corn out front the night Race brought Faith to me.

No matter how many days I still had, I was going to hang on to the vision of this bizarre night with this interesting woman. Sitting there at my table in the day's trailing glow, Race poured some cheap, bottom-shelf Mexican tequila, and we threw it back. Me, wincing. Her, swallowing, smooth and easy.

Meanwhile, the miracles were still several weeks away, waiting for all of us.

Outside, a warm breeze kicked up to sift through my window screen, to move across us. She laughed at something Race finally found the guts to say, and I heard a chime in the sound. Then she turned to me, and she smiled good and hard as if that alone would save my life.

Suddenly, I felt it. Something surrounding me, but it wasn't her raspberry scent or the surge of tequila and lime riding the air. Something huge and intense. Whatever it was, I hadn't felt this good in a long while. Since any of my three wives. Or since the spring, when all my hair wound up in the teeth of my comb, and I shut myself in from the rest of the world with nothing but chemo drips and tequila chasers. Now here was Faith Countryman. I figured this was about as close to Heaven as I'd ever get.

When it was time for her to start all that praying, and hollering, and carrying on like she did, Faith and Race helped me over to the sofa in the family room. It dawned on me that I had cultivated an impressive amount of dirt and dust in there, too. I would have apologized, but she gave me a little shove backward onto a throw pillow, then shut her eyes and lifted her face straight up toward the ceiling. Her voice grew deep and serious, and all the bells in her laugh disappeared. She held on to me with such strength that I knew there was a good chance I'd die right then and there, but then I figured it might be the best way to go.

Sniffing raspberries. Losing everything. Waiting for the light to slip out of the day.

Later, when I walked Faith out to the front porch, I saw her wipe her shoes on the doormat.

"Sorry the place was such a mess."

"The dirt won't stick to us forever, baby." She smiled and gave my hand a little squeeze. Then I felt her fingers release mine.

I often wondered about that visit. I tried to imagine what might have happened if things had been different. If she hadn't pounced on me outside the Mill that day and forced her way into my home. Into my life. If she hadn't washed my dishes. If she hadn't stopped to water the corn on her way out.

That night, I finally agreed with the doctors' prognosis. It was all touch and go from there. Touch and go. That happened to be Faith Countryman's specialty. It wasn't until later that any of it made sense. By that time, the corn wasn't the only thing coming back to life.

~

If you somehow set aside those grapefruit-sized malignant tumors, my night with Stan Jackson was nearly perfect. Race picked me up on Smith Street and drove at the speed of light, and by the time I stepped in Stan's kitchen, one miracle had already occurred. Stan's mind had somehow changed. He was open and willing now, fully accepting of what would happen to him. Of course, when you're sick as a desperate dog and staring death in its ugly face, you're gonna try anything and everything to save yourself. Even if it means finally surrendering to the Lord above. Or to some new woman in town with the church-verified spiritual gift of healing and a bunch of crazy requests.

"Put your head back, Stan," I instructed, holding on to him, leaning him backward over the kitchen sink. Carefully, I sprinkled his face and scalp with a stream of warm water. "Imagine that you're in the Jordan, with the Lord Jesus Himself holding you in His arms." I smiled and dried his smooth head with a terry-cloth placemat.

"Drink this." I filled his shot glass with Welch's grape juice. "All the way to your soul." Then I handed him a Ritz. "Eat it. Work it down into your marrow. Think of our Lord's broken body as you do it." I joined him in the ritual, chewing slowly, swilling the liquid, closing my eyes.

Darkness had begun to drape the sky in a field of lights when Stan asked, "What now?"

Race and I led him into the TV room. "Take off your shirt."

Stan lay very still on his couch. Small drops of oil drained from the bottle onto his chest and abdomen.

"It doesn't get better than this," I whispered. "Pure myrrh, cassia, calamus, cinnamon, and olive. The same exact recipe as the stuff our Lord gave Moses."

"What does the oil do?" Stan asked.

"Not one darn thing." I sniffed the woody aroma, drizzling the liquid.

He frowned. "Nothing?"

"Think of it as your line in the sand. Something to cross over. For faith purposes." The oil shimmered like a magic potion on his ghostly skin. "Before this oil, you were faithless, hopeless. But now . . ." I lightly pressed droplets on his head. "Now is your moment."

Stan blinked as he lay silent, while his bald head shone like a brilliant sphere in the moonlight.

"The only way we're gonna get you healed is with unwavering faith." Oil slowly spilled from the bottle. I whipped a prayer cloth from my waistband. "In real life, this is nothing but a dishtowel I just swiped from your kitchen drawer. But God doesn't care. He only cares about all the faith that's loaded up behind it." I covered the oil on his chest with the cloth.

"Where two or more are joined . . ." I whispered the verse softly. "Let's believe together right now." I watched Stan close his lashless eyelids. Holding his hands in mine, I began to pray in a foreign tongue, a heavenly language that Stan and I would never begin to understand.

When I opened my eyes several moments later, Stan was staring at me, dumbfounded. "Okay, Stan," I continued, "what Bible verses might you happen to know from memory?"

Completely fatigued now, all he could do was shake his head from side to side.

"Well, no wonder you've been knocking on death's door!" I tsked. "Daily meditation on our Lord's Holy Scriptures would've kept you walking in divine health all by itself. Works better than vitamins!"

Stan's skinny arm rose to grab my hand. "Wait!"

A flush of warmth coursed through me when I felt the strength in his grip.

"When I was a little kid, my grandma taught me the Twenty-Third Psalm."

"I'll bet she did."

"The Lord is my Shepherd, I shall not want . . ."

"Hallelujah." I stood to gently cover Stan with a blanket.

"Yea, though I walk through the valley of the shadow of death . . ."

I bent to plant a kiss on his forehead, like I was a woman who'd loved him true-blue for all of his days. When my lips pushed onto his withered, dry skin, I really did love him. So very much.

His voice cracked from sheer exhaustion. "You annointeth my head with oil . . ."

Stan made it through the Twenty-Third Psalm exactly three times before all the upchucking started. That's when I knew good things were happening. That Stan was regurgitating more than Ritz Communion crackers, residual Twinkies, brown rills of disgusting bile, and huge clumps of who knows what else. Wobbling on his feeble stick legs, he tried his best to escort me to the front door, but the retching kept him from standing there long enough to say his proper good-byes.

We left Stan Jackson then. In his little house all by himself. Back in the most sacred of holy positions. On his knees. At the toilet. For vomiting and prayer.

I hollered over my shoulder on the way out. "Keep reciting your grandma's psalm, Stan. Don't you dare stop. Start saying how well and healed you are right out loud, for all the world to hear. Believe it. Receive it. You say it, and then you get it."

Race held the car door for me at the curb, his eyes practically drilling holes in my face, like he'd never seen such a thing in all his life. I smiled and patted him on the arm and settled into the passenger seat.

Warm air swirled in the car window, tousling my hair as Race McGee sped through the empty avenues of Cross Creek.

"Somebody chasing us, Race?" I twisted in my seat to glance behind the Chevy. "What's the big rush?"

"Just anxious to get outta there, I guess." Race's foot was slammed to the floorboards. "That was a long night."

"You spooked or something?"

"I'm something, but I don't know exactly what." Race smiled and hairpinned the corner.

Moments later, he pressed the brake outside the Victorian.

"You're going back over there, right?"

Race nodded. "I'll keep an eye on him tonight." The car idled, vibrating loudly. "So, what's next, Faith Countryman? Handling snakes? Casting out demons?"

I laughed. "Well now, it sounds like you're a man who's dusted off his Bible a few times." I let the door slam behind me. "Next time, we're gonna ask the Good Lord to slow down your engine so you don't have to speed through this life of yours anymore."

~

Out of the silence of the morning, I was roused by the chime of timeless words inside my head. *He maketh me to lie down in green pastures.* Opening my eyes, I instantly thought of Stan Jackson, visualizing him in all of his Scripture-proclaiming, toilet-hugging splendor. Long night or not, the dawn of day brought none other than the Sabbath, and it was crystal clear what that meant. I swung my feet to the floor. No way was I going to miss Sunday service when God was moving so mightily on Stan's behalf. While I stood waiting in the wings for the full manifestation of one power-packed, miraculous stage-4 healing in the natural realm.

"Thou preparest a table before me," I murmured in the kitchen, as if in spiritual cahoots with Stan in a crosstown Scripture recitation. I broke off a piece of bran muffin and poured coffee.

"He leadeth me beside still waters." I flipped on the faucet at the bathtub, snapping my fingers to the verse's lilting rhythm.

Heat poured off the sun as I drove the narrow two-lane stretch of pavement that ascended above town. Slope to slope, I wound higher, where, as if by creative design, all of Cross Creek's churches were located. Their steeples aimed at Heaven in a unified gesture of architectural worship.

The Church on the High Hill stood highest of all. Looming bright on a golden hillside, it backed up against mountainous terrain. From there, I could see down all the way to Main Street, its surrounding neighborhoods, and even the exact location where one creek narrowed and crossed to intersect with the water that ran past the mill, making it clear as day why Cross Creek was given its name. There, in the canyon far below, a frothy liquid blue crucifix streamed, glimmering within the grassy banks.

I parked at the edge of the field grass, set the brake, and hurried toward the massive doors beneath the bell tower. I was late, but it didn't matter. Going to the Church on the High Hill felt like coming home.

TESTIMONY

PASTOR ALEXANDER MOSLEY

∼

*I*n all my years of preaching, I never saw the light fall down on my church like the day Faith Countryman showed up. The woman was positively radiant. Gospel truth. She woke us up real good one Sunday when she stepped into my sanctuary for the first time, lambent in the most extraordinary glow. One minute, the offering baskets were zigzagging through the congregation. Then lo and behold, Faith drifted in, bejeweled with colors filtered by all the stained glass.

That was precisely when the phrase "Lord, have mercy" took on new meaning in my life.

She was ten minutes late, but even on time, she would have been impossible to miss. Strangers were a rarity in Cross Creek, and strangers who dressed like sophisticated types or fashion models didn't exactly land in a church pew on Sunday morning up at the High Hill. Everyone looked shocked out of their skivvies, squirming and frowning, watching to see what might happen next. I could practically read their minds right behind their Sunday bulletins. *Where in the blazes did this lady come from?*

She removed her sunglasses and bolted straight for the front row. With a flip of her hair over her shoulder, she settled into a seat while all of High Hill's membership sat stunned. Waiting. In total silence. If someone had chosen that moment to drop the proverbial pin, we'd have heard that thing hit the floor like a bucket of nails at Spencer's Hardware.

It was my job to speak, and to actually make sense after such an unusual interruption in our service's opening moments. Only God Himself could get me through that. But it was Mrs. Marble who beat both God and me to the punch. She jumped up from the organ to introduce "Send the Light" as our next hymn. "On page 117," Mrs. Marble screeched, and threw me a look of reprimand.

"Let it shine forevermore," we sang in a hushed tone, "from shore to shore."

Out of the corner of my eye, I saw that Faith Countryman sang every single word without even one glance at the Broadman Hymnal in the crook of her arm.

That got me wondering what her story might be.

People had been telling me their stories for twenty-five years. Ever since the day I hung the "Pastor" sign on my door and plunked a box of Kleenex on my desk, I'd heard all the sins, confessions, sob stories, and weird secrets a man could care to hear. When people revealed this wacky stuff, I just nodded. I'd learned that most folks will tell you everything they ever knew as long as you kept nodding and acted like you cared.

But things could get rather ticklish when people's sins and confessions started crisscrossing each other right there in my office. Case in point—the day Jeff Gainsville plopped down in the chair. "I don't love my wife anymore," he announced and sat back, staring, waiting for some kind of fire and brimstone fallout.

"Oh yeah?" I responded like I always did to this complaint. "Well, join the club. From what I've heard, it's got an awfully large membership. Now, what can I do for you today, Jeff?"

Then that very afternoon, in came Rochelle Gainsville with a low-cut top and a highfalutin attitude. "I've been pretty upset with Jeff lately," she drawled as she tapped her long fingernails on my Bible concordance.

I nodded and pushed the Kleenex box her way. I knew what was coming. The weird secret part.

"When I'm really ticked, I wait for Jeff to drive to town. Then I take his toothbrush, and I scrub the toilet with it like there's no tomorrow. When I'm done, I just give it a little shake and put it back in his drawer like nothing's ever happened. 'Course, I try not French-kissing him for a while."

I stared at her, slack-jawed.

"Oh, he deserves it." She blew her nose at me with a honk.

After these sorry souls spilled their beans in my office chambers, they always wanted the same thing. The answer to their biggest question. Were they getting in or not? Into Heaven. This was where I always asked one question right back. Was there a time or a moment that stopped them in their tracks, dropped them to their knees, or maybe sent a chill running all the way up their backs? Perhaps they heard themselves say out loud, "Okay, Jesus, I get it. Yup. Hallelujah."

Now, once that question was out there, I had to have my eyes peeled, because nine times out of ten, I could tell who would make the cut in the hereafter. If they'd truly experienced a soul-saving episode, the light would manifest right then and there. I'd see it plain as day. On them or coming out of them. Sometimes, it was a knowing look in their eyes. A flicker that moved real slow across their expressions.

It always came down to the very same thing our Creator started off with in the first place. Light.

I don't know what got into me the day Faith Countryman walked into our lives, but Lord knows, I never preached a sermon like that one before. The message came from the Gospel of Luke, when Jesus had His feet washed by a sinful woman. Well, those uppity, belly-aching Pharisees eyewitnessed the foot bath. Jesus read their minds, then said a powerful thing, "Hey, you guys didn't even bother to greet me. But this woman has washed my feet with her tears, and wiped them dry with her hair." Then He continued. "Okay, she's a huge sinner, but only a person who's been enormously forgiven can turn around and love a Savior like this." I paused for evangelistic effect. "Well, folks, you know what our Lord did then? He set that woman free! From her past. From all of her sins. Just like that!" I snapped my fingers, waking up Bob Benson in the third row.

Immediately after the sermon, Faith Countryman was the first one to jump up at the altar call, walk to the front, and make a personal decision for the Lord.

Moments later, we shook hands at the sanctuary doors out on the front steps.

"Glad to be a part of your saving day, miss," I told her.

"Rededication, Pastor," she corrected me, adjusting her sunglasses up the bridge of her nose. "It's something I like to do regularly. Just to keep things in check."

I nodded, waiting for her to continue.

"I'm one of the lucky ones," she whispered as she leaned in. Then she turned to see what I thought about that.

And there it was. That look I'd come to recognize after years in the Lord's service. With all the light you could ever imagine. This time, glowing with extraordinary brilliance. I watched it brighten her entire expression before it rolled across her face.

"You know what I mean, Pastor," she said softly. "I'm one of the chosen ones. That's what the Good Book says, right? That, ultimately, it's God who chooses us, and not the other way around."

"Well, uh, yeah, I suppose you're right."

"You know I am." She laughed. "But let me tell you something else."

I stepped closer to hear, wondering what might be coming next. The smell of her was like fresh sliced tangerine.

"While everyone in the world is just trying to believe or prove that God exists, I have done nothing but love Him since I was the smallest little *child." Her words poured out in an exhale. "Don't get me wrong, I've done my share of sinning." She looked over her sunglasses at me. "But like that wet-haired woman in the book of Luke, understanding forgiveness just makes me love Him all the more."*

Standing there on my church steps, under a steeple you can see for miles, I watched a single tear roll down her cheek and drop off her jaw.

"What brings you to Cross Creek?" I finally asked.

"Now, that is some story." She smiled, examining the view off our high hill in every direction. "Mostly, I'm here to take care of a little business."

That Sunday morning, with the sun spilled over her like a glittering dew, Faith Countryman taught me a big lesson. You see, sometimes a preacher will forget what on earth he's supposed to be talking about. He'll lecture religion for so long, he doesn't even realize when things have gone cold and dark on him. Then one day something happens, everything shifts, and in order to save his own self, he makes a break for the most spectacular thing around. For whatever's casting the brightest glow. Gospel truth.

Later that summer, when everyone was thinking about her, I always remembered my first impression. When the church doors opened, and the light cut through. When the winds of change blew her straight into one of my pews, already knowing all the songs by heart.

∾

Having friends in high places was better than a kick in the teeth any old day. By the time I left Pastor Mosley at the Church on the High Hill, I held a slip of paper with the names of a telephone serviceman, a television/cable technician, and a real estate agent. Along with Mosley's assurance that none of them would mind being bothered on a Sunday, despite most small-town churchgoers believing that work done on the Sabbath was one sneeze away from a criminal act.

It didn't hurt to have friends across the street either. Since I needed to borrow a telephone, I tapped on the Merriweathers' door. Within seconds, out came a woman dusted with flour and wearing oven mitts.

"Faith Countryman." She shook her head. "Would you believe there's a peach pie coming out of the oven right now with your name on it?"

"Mrs. Merriweather?"

"Call me Lucinda. My boys told me all about you."

I shook hands with her sticky oven mitt. "Nice to meet you, Lucinda."

"The pie is my way of saying thanks for sharing your talents on the piano with us these past few nights."

"Talents? Oh, I'm just messing around mostly."

"True to the bone, girl, your piano playing has changed the whole atmosphere here on Smith Street."

Except for a fine mist of white flour, the Merriweather kitchen was clean as a whistle. Lucinda swung open the oven door. "Your pie is ready," she whispered, carefully cradling the hot dessert to the countertop.

"Wow. I might have to come visit you regularly, Lucinda." I smiled. "Just so you know, I pretty much flunked all my formal piano lessons."

"No!" Lucinda slammed the oven door shut.

I nodded. "I play entirely by ear."

"With those little things?" She winked and pointed at my ears. "I'll have to see that someday." She chuckled, and flung off her oven mitts.

Shocked, I watched her ten gnarled fingers curl out to point in different directions.

Seeing my reaction, Lucinda instantly commented, "Oh, honey, don't mind these. I've had arthritis since before you were born." She rubbed her hands together. "Funny thing, though, my old fingers have been feeling so good lately. I can't figure it out. I finished my needlepoint in record time the other night. All the while listening to your piano."

The Holy Spirit didn't need to poke me with a stick on this one. Reaching for Lucinda's lumpy fingers, I silently made requests on her behalf, calling for healing, straight fingers, no pain, the feeling of agility and youth. All of this I lifted up, to mingle on the air with sugary peaches and nutmeg and cinnamon.

When I opened my eyes, Lucinda was studying me.

"It's been nice having some life in that old Victorian again." Her voice was sincere.

"It's such a beautiful place. I wish I could stay there."

Lucinda waited.

"But I can't."

Lucinda waited longer.

"I need to sell it and go back home."

Lucinda stared at me.

"Back to where I belong and all."

Lucinda smiled as if she had a secret.

I thought about that secret smile of hers after I made my phone calls, when I walked back across the street to eat the biggest, most decadent piece of warm peach pie I'd ever consumed in one sitting.

And that woman thought *I* had talent?

Late in the day, with a dial tone, a TV signal, and an appointment to meet with a real estate agent, I set out on a walk with Solomon. We ended up at the dock at Creekside Park with a woman whose kids hung on the jungle gym like chimpanzees at feeding time.

It was a beautiful night. Cross Creek wouldn't have been a half-bad place to stay to live if I didn't really need to get home again someday.

TESTIMONY

PAM PARKER

~

*T*he first time I saw Faith Countryman, she made me sick to my stomach. Newcomers never did sit well with me. It was hard enough trusting the folks you already knew, let alone some stranger sneaking up on you.

"Well, well, well. Would you get a load of Miss Hot Stuff!" I muttered under my breath.

The kids and I were hanging out at Creekside Park, where Faith had stretched out on the dock with her big yellow dog. She was smiley and smug, acting like anybody could sashay into town, slide into that Victorian on Smith Street, and traipse around without a care. Self-assurance dripped off of her like summer sweat off a combine driver.

"Totally nauseating," I whispered to myself.

In order to smile and be smug and carefree like Faith Countryman, I would've needed a lobotomy. To forget all the ugly things. Even in the best moments when I watched my kids giggle and run their long skinny legs to the creek, or when my husband, Travis, gave me that look like we were *seventeen again, the crash always came. At break-neck speed, too. Our boys would pitch their laughter higher than the treetops. Daisy would whisper up at me from tall grass with her little-girl eyes. But all I could hear was my own voice. Screaming. Absolutely terrified. Bouncing off the walls on the inside of my head.*

Faith Countryman pulled a big book out of her backpack. It looked like a Bible with its leather cover and tissue pages. Imagine that, I snickered to myself. A woman like her needing God, or the Bible. What a wacko.

"Even I don't need God, and I've had my full share of problems in life," I mumbled.

Out the corner of my eye, I noticed her khaki shorts, white T-shirt, and sandals. My fashion statement might have been described as mustard-smudged stretch pants paired with worn-out loafers, accessorized by a trio of stringy-haired kids who screamed like banshees. That very minute, two of my little ones were on swings, waiting for pushes, hollering for me, as if saying it a hundred times was gonna do the trick.

"Push us, Mommy!"

"Mommy! Pleeeeease!"

Over on the monkey bars and hanging upside down was my eldest, Ronnie, practicing Dr. Pepper burps like somebody was about to hand out a prize for the most disgusting one.

I shuffled through the sand to push my two youngest, Ricky and Daisy, when, out of nowhere, Faith Countryman stood up, walked the planks of the dock, and headed straight for me.

"There you are!" she called out with a wave.

I glanced behind me. Who was she talking to? I turned back to my kids.

"I was wondering when I'd find you," she said, looking right at me.

A split second later, Ronnie flew off the monkey bars and landed cock-eyed on his arm. And quicker than you could ask "Is there a doctor of orthopedics in the house?" this little blond Bible-thumper was on him. Completely taking over, she held Ronnie in her arms, urgently whispering to "my Lord Jesus" as if He was exclusively hers. I watched her cradle Ronnie's ill-bent arm while my other two kids hollered and hung on to my legs like a couple of wet blankets. Shaking off my little ones, I lunged for Ronnie, imagining his trauma. But doggone it, he was all goofy looking, smiling up at his rescuer with this weird expression on his face.

"Hey!" I yelled. "Lady, what do you think you're doing?"

Right then, Faith touched me. "What's your name?" she asked with a big smile on her face.

I shook my head and tried to pull free of her, but she grabbed on to me even tighter.

"Help me out here, Mom. Now, what's your name?"

"Pam."

"Well, Pam, it's time to say 'praise the Lord' or whatever it is you would usually say to our Heavenly Father."

"I would usually say absolutely nothing."

Good. Now she knew I was a smartass.

She smiled right through me. "Okay then, say nothing, but shut your eyes and get on your knees while you're at it."

With that, she gently shoved me, and down I went, till my kneecaps landed softly in the sand.

"And being that this here's your boy, Pam, don't screw things up, okay?"

I liked that. Her being a bit sassy, too.

Faith watched me for a moment, as if she could hear those screams inside my head. Then she kept right on talking with Ronnie. Or with God. Or whoever she thought she was talking to.

Within moments, Ronnie was back on the monkey bars. "Thanks, Faith. It feels great." He stretched out his arm and waved.

Something tickled its way up my spine, all the way from the elastic of my stretch pants to the nape of my neck.

"I knew we'd be friends, Pam," Faith observed as Ronnie gripped the bar. "I could tell the moment I laid eyes on you."

That evening, as the night darkened around a glowy moon, Faith and I dangled our toes off the dock, and I began to learn all about her. Where she'd come from. Where she'd been. Her plans to sell the Victorian and go home. That she smelled like sweet apples in the sun, even in the pitch black of night.

"What's that perfume you're wearing, Faith?"

"None at all."

"You smell like a Golden Delicious."

"Fruits of the Spirit, maybe?" She laughed. "Funny how things manifest."

When she mentioned she needed a summer job, I stuck my nose right into her business and told her about Harley Stone, and the most beautiful ranch in Cross Creek.

Later that night, I dumped my loafers and stretch pants in the garbage can, and I began to shed the extra pounds that had snuck up on me since Daisy came along. Later that summer, some of the guys told Travis that I looked as good as I did back in high school. When it was us giggling with skinny legs, young and free, running around down at the river. When life was easy.

For everyone except me.

By the time all of the screaming inside my head finally stopped, Faith Countryman and I were close friends. Even then, she still managed to freak me out.

If there was a sight for sore eyes in Cross Creek, Pam Parker had detailed instructions for seeing it.

"Get yourself over to Stone Ranch," she advised that night at the park. "When you arrive, close out the rest of the world. Take in the view." She promised a sight so amazing, it would simultaneously bowl me over and knock my socks off. "Harley Stone always has work." Pam had nodded. "And he is one good man." She let out a sigh that practically turned into a moan. "I don't even know how to describe his kind of goodness. Trust me. You're gonna have to see things for yourself."

But seeing things for myself had to wait until I'd polished every nook and cranny of the Victorian to prepare it for prospective buyers. And after I'd explored the area's walking trails and the shops along Main Street.

A few weeks later, with curiosity but no clue whatsoever, I ventured out with Solomon. We went early to beat the heat, walking first through Cross Creek's quiet town center, then miles back into the lower foothills. Past the six-mile marker, to the right at the split in the woodsy patch, and beyond the three-sided crumbly orange barn. When the river rushed beside us, I found the gate made of stone pillars and wooden beams. It was opened wide to what appeared to be 7 River Road.

Then I remembered Pam's advice.

With fresh air filling my lungs and sunlight warm on my face, I opened myself to the scene before me. Beyond the gate, a pebbled driveway stretched out a long straight path. When the thicket of leafy aspens broke clear, a ranch suddenly emerged to sprawl across the valley floor and climb the sloping grade. With orchards of olive trees, an expansive grape vineyard, a portion of the river cutting through, and a three-story ranch house set in the basin, beauty drenched the landscape in every direction. Best of all, Stone Ranch sat tucked in at the deepest cut of the hillside, hidden from the rest of the world.

TESTIMONY

HARLEY STONE

~

*I*t was the end of June. Blazing hot. The first day of the season's heat wave, too, ushered in by a minor emergency that erupted and blew apart my morning.

"Harley!" my ranch foreman, Al, shouted through the kitchen window screen.

It was way too early for whatever had him going like a maniac, already running up the slope.

"Spigot's finally let go! Thing's shooting water clear to the moon!"

"No way," I muttered, shifting from coffee and the newspaper to instant high gear.

As soon as I charged off the porch, it hit me—thick air loaded with sky-rocketing temperature, letting loose a mixture of odors. Alfalfa, eucalyptus, and just-turned soil. Running past the cat, I looked back to make sure she wasn't dead, draped over the windowsill like that. Then past the birds, who took cover under the maple leaves.

Straight up to the barn full tilt, I ripped through the place looking for my adjustable wrench and hacksaw. I found my long-lost San Francisco 49er's sweatshirt and an old steering wheel from a truck I didn't remember, but no sign of the tools I needed right then.

Smoke, my black Lab, decided to join in the ruckus. He was full of it, too, yapping up a storm outside. His barking went on for a good while, and seemed to grow louder by the minute. Finally, I stopped digging in the tool cupboard long enough to go see what his fussing was about. Rounding the corner of the barn, I squinted into the sunlight.

And there she was.

From the looks of it, she was in a bit of a bind, too. She and her big gold dog were being circled by Smoke, who, after all his years of slacking on the job, had suddenly decided to be a guard dog.

"Smoke! Knock it off!" I watched him back down, growling and wagging his tail at the same time. "Sit, Smoke. Stay. Stay right there."

Smoke calmed down. He and the gold dog sniffed each other, and soon enough, both tails were wagging.

"Sorry about that!" the woman called up to me. "We didn't mean to get everybody all riled up."

I knew exactly who she was. In town only a few weeks, but everyone was aware of her. I'd seen her shopping at the Mill when she'd first arrived, and sightings of her were the new topic of conversation.

"Sorry to barge in on you like this. I'm guessing this is 7 River Road, right?" She started up the slope toward me. "I didn't see a marker."

"This is it." I headed down to meet her.

"I'm Faith Countryman."

"Hi, Faith. I'd shake your hand, but I've been digging through the barn and . . . oh!" I whipped around to get a full view of the upper field. My crew had managed to shut off the water. And there was Al, calmed down now, talking to one of the guys holding both the wrench and the hacksaw I'd just knocked myself out trying to find.

I shook my head and turned back to Faith.

"Everything okay?" She asked.

"Yeah." I laughed. "I'm Harley Stone."

Never mind all the grimy barn dust; she took a firm hold of my hand anyway. And that was pretty much that. From then on, things were never really the same.

Turns out, she was looking for a job. She'd walked the whole way from Smith Street to inquire about it. "About six miles, right?" she asked, taking a deep breath, energized from her trek.

I nodded. "Sounds about right."

I was blown away. I'd put up a help-wanted notice at the drug store three months ago, and this time, not one person had called to ask about it. Not the church ladies, the friends' wives, the teenage kids looking for summer jobs. Not even slutty old Judi Ward, for crying out loud. Then suddenly, first thing in the morning, this woman shows up.

Of course, she was absolutely dead wrong for this. It was an ugly job. With enormous responsibility and a monotonous drudgery. She obviously had no idea.

"Faith, what I've got here is no picnic. By the time you'd settle into the routine and the work, and there's plenty of both of those, well, you'd most likely be looking for the door."

That was only half of it. Truth was, she was something. The kind of something that walking six miles up a gradual incline in the heat didn't even begin to dent. She hadn't even broken a sweat. No matter who Faith Countryman was, or what the heck she was doing here, I knew I didn't want some woman like her getting a close-up view of my life.

"Harley, you're not scaring me," she objected. "I was raised on a ranch. I know how these things go. I'm sure I'll handle it just fine."

Okay, maybe it was just me, but all of a sudden everything seemed to gear down to slow motion. As if time had finally up and decided to switch to a crawl, so I could stop running, stop working, stop jamming and slamming.

I gave it one more shot. I described the cleaning, the cooking, all the mundane stuff. The long hours. Everything.

She tapped me on the shoulder. "Harley, we can go back and forth like this for as long as you want. But in the end, I think you're gonna wind up giving me a try."

I took a deep breath. "Okay, Faith. Let's do it."

By the time summer was in full swing, there were people all over our little town just wishing for a few seconds of her time, and I still had her on my ranch with me every day. It was an incredible feeling, though not nearly as wild as learning about her and appreciating her friendship, and, okay, nearly falling for her, like some other guy might have.

But I wasn't like some other guy.

That first day, after Faith had gone home, I asked my wife, Samantha, what she thought of her.

Samantha struggled to answer, but all she could do was blink twice.

That summer, I just put my head down and kept working. If it didn't need fixing, I was the guy who went ahead and fixed it anyway. If I burned myself out long enough looping wire in the vineyard, or took my sweet time plowing the bottom acres, maybe I could keep clear of the house. If I revised the irrigation system to perfection, repaired planks on the barn and threw new paint on it, or fixed the leaky sink in the upstairs bathroom, maybe I could keep busy enough to stay away from her. Maybe I could sleep at night. My crew couldn't figure out what had gotten into me. They said the ranch was in the best shape they'd ever seen. They urged me to go on vacation, take a few days off, a week or two even. Then one morning they saw me walking up River Road with Faith Countryman at my side, and they never mentioned it again.

Some days, I'd sit under the oaks up on the ridge and look out across my land, holding my breath, watching for movement at the turn of the road. Despite the fact that one of my lifelong intentions was to steer clear of hot water, I knew I'd started boiling myself in a big pot of it the moment Faith Countryman walked the tail end of that six-mile stretch straight into my life.

With all those brothers of mine, I knew exactly how things go haywire and hogwash anytime a man is left in charge of a home's insides. With this in mind, I followed Harley Stone into his mansion of a ranch house. Through the double doors and onto the shiny wood floors of his entry hall. I found myself hugely surprised.

"Time to see what you're getting into." Harley led the way.

So far, what I was getting into looked pretty darn impressive. A little dust and clutter, but overall, no one would have ever guessed that the man of the house had been taking care of things by himself.

"I've had help off and on. Not lately, though."

"How long has it been?"

"Since the start? Nine years." He paused. "Nine years, ten months, and a couple of weeks. But who's counting, right?" He flashed a grin, then turned his back to lead the way down a wide corridor.

And thank goodness for that, because I almost choked to death trying to catch my next breath. Holy smokes! Had this man's smile actually shaken me? It was hard to tell, because he had a confident kind of walk that could really get your attention, too. I'd almost forgotten these details from that day in the produce section at the Mill, but now, as I trailed him down the hallway, I was reminded of his demeanor. Along with the fact that he was very nice looking, with dark brown hair, and even darker eyes, and olive skin. What was my new friend Pam thinking, sending me over here for a job, encouraging me to "see things for myself"?

Harley glanced over his shoulder to make sure I was keeping up. "This way, Faith."

We entered the living room where the sunlight blasted through a wall of windows that overlooked the river. Where my breath caught when I saw her for the first time.

"Here she is." Harley lowered his voice. "This is my wife. Samantha."

"Your wife?" I tried not gulping the words.

Samantha sat. Asleep in her wheelchair.

She was a beauty. Completely covered in brilliant yellows streaking through the glass. With her black hair swept up in a barrette, revealing the curve of her cheekbones and the full line of her pinkish lips.

"This is where she spends her mornings," Harley whispered, approaching her chair. He quickly scanned her from head to toe, then watched her carefully for a minute, studying her sleeping face.

I waited, feeling the sunlight warm the room.

Harley went on to check her breathing and pulse. He adjusted her pillow and pushed back a strand of hair from her face. He set her feet straight on the footrest and smoothed her rumpled clothing.

He stepped back, turning to me. "We have a nurse who comes in every day. To monitor and watch her, bathe her, give her her medicine, help with exercises and physical therapy. I'll just need you to keep an eye on her here and there."

"All right."

"She sits mostly. Or sleeps. All day."

Close up, Samantha looked serene. Her fingernails were clean, trimmed, and painted. The air from a nearby fan blew lightly on her delicate features. She would have been a knockout if fate had placed her in different circumstances. Or in some other mode of transportation. She would've looked fantastic climbing out of a sports car, stepping on her own two feet, trying to keep pace with her handsome husband.

"Samantha was in a plane crash when Kyle was a baby."

"Kyle?"

"Our son."

"Oh."

"He's ten. He's at a friend's house right now."

I nodded.

"The pilot died on impact. They said it was a miracle she survived." Harley leaned against the windowsill. "But I think miracles are not always meant to be."

My words came out before I could think. "No, Harley," I said softly. "Miracles are always meant to be."

Harley looked out the window where a pepper tree bowed its limb in the breeze. Beyond that, a striped umbrella shaded a chaise lounge on a redwood sundeck next to the creek.

"Her damage is extensive. She doesn't walk or talk." Harley paused. "It's hard to tell what's on her mind. If anything."

Framed photographs lined the walls around us. The raven-haired woman who smiled from under the glass was a stunning bride. Dazzling as she lounged in a ski boat. Adorable eating an ice cream cone, and cradling a baby in her arms.

Harley tapped his wife's hand. "Samantha, we've got company. This is Faith Countryman. She's going to be helping us with the house, and with you and Kyle."

Samantha slowly opened her eyes, then began to blink rapidly.

Stooping down, I held both of her hands and greeted her. "Hi, Samantha."

Her navy blue eyes connected with mine.

Harley continued. "The nurse usually gets here around nine."

"Okay. So, along with keeping an eye on Samantha and Kyle, what else needs to be done?"

"There's laundry, cleaning, and grocery shopping."

"Sounds easy enough."

"When can you start?"

"Right now, if you want me to."

"I was hoping you'd say that. This place could really use it."

"Wait, aren't you the guy who tried talking me out of this job a few minutes ago?"

I watched Harley laugh and walk out of the room. When I turned back, Samantha's dark eyes were latched on to mine.

"How about a change of scenery, Samantha?" I pushed her chair into the Stones' elaborate country kitchen, located the sponge, and started soaping up the counters. After I'd wiped everything dry and shut off the faucet, I heard a sound behind me. A boy with hair as white as could be stood at the doorway.

"Hi." I smiled, drying my hands on a dishtowel. "You must be Kyle Stone."

"Yes, ma'am."

"I'm Faith. Your dad asked me to help you guys around the house for a while."

"Oh."

"Did you have a good time at your friend's house?"

"Yeah."

Kyle sat in the chair next to his mom and patted her hand. Samantha blinked twice.

"When she blinks two times, that means yes, or good, or okay." Kyle informed me. "Other than that, she just stares a lot."

"But the two of you have your own language, huh? With those double blinks?"

"Yep, but she can stare forever. She'll beat you in a stare-out contest every time."

"I won't be messing with her on that, then."

With a notepad and pen, I began a grocery list. "What are some of your favorite foods, Kyle?"

Kyle shrugged politely, but after some coaxing, he admitted to Jell-O, spaghetti and meatballs, brownies, and root beer. Soon, I had a full page of items scribbled.

"Tomorrow, you'll have lots of good stuff stocked in your fridge."

"Thanks, Faith."

He ran to grab two fishing poles off the porch and join his dad on the sundeck at the edge of the river.

As I folded the last load of laundry, I watched them: Kyle, looking excited, way too antsy to wait around for fish to bite. Harley, seeming talkative, conversing often, bending over Kyle's line to check the bait, finally feeling a tug, handing the pole back to Kyle, encouraging his son to bring in his catch.

By the time the sun had begun to glide down the hill beyond the water, the fish had been tossed back. The nurse had come and gone. Samantha was asleep in her wheelchair again. Kyle was watching TV. The kitchen, breakfast nook, dining room, and service porch were tidy and scrubbed clean. A tuna salad with sweet pickle relish sat in the fridge for the Stones' dinner. If I was going to walk all the way back to Smith Street and shop at the Mill before it closed, I needed to get going.

At the doorway, I pointed my finger at Kyle. "Okay, Jell-O, spaghetti and meatballs, brownies, and . . ." I snapped my fingers, teasing. "Um, oh yeah . . . beer."

His eyes widened. "No, *root* beer."

"Oh, that's right." I gave him a wink.

Outside the screen door, Solomon and Smoke were nose to nose, sharing the porch. But Harley was nowhere in sight.

"Hey, Kyle," I called through the screen. "Do you think I need to wait for your dad? Or can I leave you and your mom alone?"

"You can go. I've watched my mom a million times. Besides, Dad's probably in hollering distance."

Solomon and I had just passed the curve in River Road when Harley caught up to us in his truck. He slowed and leaned across the seat to push open the passenger door.

"Hop in, Faith."

"You sure?"

"After you walked to my place this morning, then worked all day? You'll keel over if you try walking back now. You might not come back tomorrow."

He waited for me to decide. With his arms draped over the steering wheel, he looked like he had all the time in the world to sit there and talk me into this.

But I knew better. The work was piled sky high for this man.

"Trust me." I secured the tailgate for Solomon and climbed in next to Harley. "I've never called in sick a day in my life."

His smile snuck up on me then, right out from under his worn-out baseball cap and aviator sunglasses. He pushed on the gas and wound us the back way into Cross Creek, pulling up Smith Street to my front curb.

"See you tomorrow, Harley."

"Thanks for coming over to help us out, Faith."

I didn't dare look back at him. Not this man. Not with his wife and his son and his big beautiful home in the grassy canyon next to the hills. Not with his kind of goodness. Harley wasn't even down the street before I couldn't wait to get back to Stone Ranch to get that place in shape.

～

The Mill Grocery and Grain Supply was so quiet, you could hear the river out back, lapping up against the rocks. I stepped in with the

Stones' grocery list just as the lights dimmed for closing time. A lone cashier gave me a weary smile before glancing at his watch.

Scurrying by, I offered my apology. "I'll be quick about it, I promise."

"Take your time, ma'am," he lied graciously, then reburied his nose in the *National Enquirer*.

I began to fill the cart, trying to sort out all the clutter in my head. *Harley Stone is married.*

Now, I knew good and well that temptations had a way of hooking on and wiggling down into your empty spots. They were like quicksand, gooey strongholds to be instantly rebuked in order to keep from getting sucked into something that could smother you alive. This Harley Stone matter was no exception.

And by the way, too late now. 'Cause I'd begged, insisted, and locked myself right into this job. I'd met the whole family, too, and was armed with their personal shopping list now. Besides, it was just for the summer, and time had a way of flying by.

I measured a bundle of fresh apricots in the scale, then scooped them into a produce box.

Harley Stone is married.

Those words continued to echo, followed by a clear memory of Mama, a woman with the grand total of zero patience for marital calamities, or anything resembling coveting that which belonged to someone else. According to her, a wandering eye was to be poked out. A cheating husband was to be strung up by his you-know-whats. That flimsy midlife crisis excuse for carrying on? Are you kidding? For a ranch woman like Mama, who could simultaneously fan off a hot flash, wash a dog, bake a chicken, hoe a row, and quote the Reverend Billy Graham while threading a needle with her tongue?

I shook my head, adding two loaves of bread to the growing grocery pile.

Harley Stone is married.

No problem at all. I would keep a good distance. I would respect their entire situation, all the while offering the best care possible for Samantha and Kyle and their home. Case closed. Besides, if there was ever a man who did not need another ounce of pressure added to his already filled-up, obligation-packed, hard-working life, it was Harley Stone.

~

Well, holy cow, Jesus, Joseph, Mary, and everybody else in the manger scene! I woke up the next morning, anxiety riddled, and downright scared that I had to go back to work for those people at that big ranch again.

Throwing off the sheets, I dove before my praying table, where candles of various shapes, colors, and essences sat next to the window. Kneeling, I watched the last bit of night melt away. My room became an altar of light, a warm pool of silent calm.

My whispers began.

"I praise You."

I struck a match and watched the fire snap the waxy wicks.

"You are the One and Only."

I bowed.

"Your deeds are mighty and wonderful."

I lifted my eyes to the ceiling.

"Who am I, that You would show me such favor?"

I shook my head.

"Such power and love."

My eyelids closed.

"I worship You with my innermost being."

Moving to a prostrate position, I lay on the rug, allowing the tears to spill.

"My sins are too many to count."

I slowly breathed in.

"Fill me with your Spirit."

In a single exhale, I released guilt and condemnation.

"Use me."

Something calmed deep inside of me.

"And please give healing to the Stones and to the good people of Cross Creek."

I sniffed and wiped my face.

My body trembled as I clearly envisioned them. Stan Jackson, with meat on his bones, speaking the words of the Twenty-Third Psalm for the thousandth time. Ronnie Parker, sleeping in his bed, feeling fine after rolling over on his arm. Lucinda Merriweather, humming in her kitchen, stretching her fingers around a teacup. Pastor Mosley under the lamplight, planning next Sunday's sermon. Samantha, with her sorrowful deep-sea eyes. And Harley, walking across his land.

When I opened my eyes, light flooded the room, and I knew it would be one spectacular day.

~

Driving my truck around the bend on River Road at the entrance to Stone Ranch, the not-so-spectacular thought hit me. Here I was, a grown woman, taking on the job of maid, babysitter, and bedside candy striper, none of which were dream positions by anyone's definition. But there I went anyway, parking beside the Stones' velvety green lawn, stepping out next to some fire-red geraniums. And here came Harley, up from the river's edge to pull all the grocery bags out of my truck.

"Morning, Faith."

I took a deep breath. "Morning, Harley. I hope you and Kyle are hungry. I've got plenty of food for you."

"Tofu and rice cakes?"

"Huh?" I gasped. "You're kidding, right?"

Harley smiled over an armload of brown bags. "Those guys at the Mill wouldn't know tofu if it hit them in the face." He propped open the screen door with his work boot. "I know I wouldn't."

"You're not missing anything."

Harley held the groceries and the door. "That's what I figured."

Seeing the Stones' kitchen for the second time, I was once again stunned by its beauty. With an oversized farm table, double-door walk-in pantry, and fireplace with brick hearth, the room was designed for family memories. But then somebody had gone and thrown a monkey wrench in the mixing bowl, and the result was that shimmering steel wheelchair perched in the middle of the room where Samantha slumped, fast asleep.

"I keep propping up her head, but she's tired today." Harley gently moved her to a straightened position.

Samantha was still in her pajamas with her hair tangled up in a royal mess.

"Ah."

"She had a rough night."

"That's too bad."

Harley peered into a couple of the bags. "Let's see, T-bones, chops, chicken, corn, pancake mix, rolls, fruit, ice cream, potatoes. Yep, that's us, all right."

"Kyle helped me with the grocery list." I looked out the window over the sink. "It's gorgeous out here today." Harley stepped closer to follow my gaze. "Right there." He nodded, gesturing up the slope. "That ridge, where the oaks line up, that's where the wind comes barreling down every winter. I could sit there all day."

"That's the spot, huh?"

Harley checked Samantha again, whose head had flopped down once more.

"I gotta get going." Harley eyed the clock. "The crew's probably wondering where I am." He grabbed an apple out of one of the bags. "Thanks again for the groceries, Faith."

"Sure thing."

The back door closed. Harley's footsteps scraped the planks of the porch, then the cement and dirt paths, finally fading to quiet. Through the nook's bay window, I saw him walk the hill to the barn. Out with the toolbox, a utility belt slung over his shoulder. He tossed the tools in the truck and slid behind the wheel. With a glance back at the house, and a mist of dust spitting from the treads, he was gone.

I turned around. Samantha's head was up now and her eyes were wide open. She was watching me like she knew exactly what was going on. In this world, on this ranch, and in this house. Like she could almost see all that quicksand I was trying my best to keep away from.

⌇

Carefully gripping Samantha's chair, I wheeled her onto River Road with the intention of walking its entire length before the heat slapped us silly. It didn't really matter that Samantha still wore her polka dot pajamas with the bed-pillow hairdo. From what I could tell, no one but Harley and his crew and the nurse ever drove down River Road, anyway.

"Here we go, Samantha."

As soon as Solomon and Smoke caught wind of our plan, they began to jog alongside.

"Breathe in that fresh air." I squeezed Samantha's shoulder.

A car suddenly appeared at the farthest end of the road and finally made its way to us next to a thicket of wild honeysuckle. Its driver was none other than Pastor Alexander Mosley from the Church on the High Hill. I almost didn't recognize him wearing too tight of a suit, seat-belted into a shiny Lincoln Continental.

"Good morning, Miss Countryman. Mrs. Stone."

"Morning, Pastor. Beautiful car you got there. Somebody get saved and tithe it to you?"

He laughed. "Well, how else does a preacher get a new car?"

"What brings you out here today?"

"You."

"Me?"

His expression sobered. "Stan Jackson has taken ill again. Things are extremely grim. He's asking for you."

"Oh no!"

"Yep. He's sure not to make it this time." Mosley dabbed at his perspiring face with a handkerchief.

"No!" I kicked the brake on Samantha's chair, giving her a little jolt. Solomon and Smoke poked up their ears. Mosley frowned as I strode to the window of the Lincoln.

"I'm sorry, Miss Countryman. He appears to be on his last leg."

"Pastor! Don't talk like that! Those are nothing but faithless words you're releasing out into the world!"

Mosley's eyes widened. "I . . . I'm sorry, but he is in the hospital one county over for complications of pneumonia. I must, at least, say that."

"Hey!" My anger rose as I leaned toward him. "This man got healed. I was with him. I felt it."

Mosley nodded. "Stan told me how you prayed for him. Very sweet of you, dear. The doctors pronounced him in remission soon after. Even going so far as to call it a miracle. But now, things are bad. Worse than ever."

"No way!" I stepped back, shaking my head. "I flat out refuse this, Pastor. Something's happened here. Someone broke the chain of faith. Destroyed the line of protection and divine healing. Someone let in doubt, and now it's run amuck."

He hanky-dabbed his forehead again, finally confessing, "Well, he and I did have a talk the other night."

I waited. "And?"

"I explained to Mr. Jackson that healings were performed all over the place back when our Lord walked the earth. But now, well . . ."

My head cocked at an angle. "Now, what?"

"Come on, Miss Countryman, do you really think God reaches all the way down from Heaven and heals people today? Right here in our little town?"

I gasped.

"I don't mean to laugh, but . . ."

I clamped shut my eyes and lifted my hand straight into the air. "Dear Lord, slap a revocation on this man's preaching license, and stuff a sock in his mouth while you're at it! Thank you, Jesus."

I flung open the driver's door, jerked Mosley out by the skintight arm of his suit, and wrestled him to his knees. "Get down here, right now. And by the way, shame on you!"

"Uh, what?"

I held him down, not letting him budge. "Please, tell me this is real to you, Pastor. That you're not some half-baked hypocrite faker making a living off the offering basket!"

"No, and if the truth be known, a church mouse couldn't live off our measly offering basket. It's just that you can't . . ."

"Shhh! You're liable to kill us with those negative confessions." I sighed. "Come on now, let's do a good thing here, Pastor." I gripped his hand, Samantha's, too, and then bowed my head. "Lord, it's me again. This time, I'm lifting up every single ill person that we know."

Samantha's pulse raced in my hand.

"Injured, diseased, broken for other reasons, it doesn't matter. Just line them up and cradle them in your unfailing love. But I especially beg you to heal Mr. Stan Jackson in that hospital one county over of what some snooty doctor with a fancy medical degree has proclaimed complications of pneumonia. Hmmph! We'll just see about that!"

"Yes, Lord," Mosley agreed in a whisper.

Samantha's grip suddenly strengthened around my own.

"Lord, none of this needs to make sense to us. The intricacies of disease, they don't matter one bit. The only thing that matters is our belief in You."

Samantha's hand went soft and limp again.

"And right now, we believe." I gripped Samantha's fingers.

"Amen." Mosley stood up and cleared his throat. With a slap at the dirt on his slacks and a pat on Samantha's head, Mosley stuffed his soggy hanky into his pocket and squeezed himself behind the steering wheel again. He left us then, in the heat and the honeysuckle, with me scowling after him all the way down River Road.

A sinking feeling came over me when I spotted the second car.

"Samantha, I'm sorry. It was never my intention to have people other than your own family witness you gallivanting around in your pajamas today."

This time, the driver was Race McGee in his lifted Chevy, moving at a speed that might have flattened us had he paid any less attention at the wheel.

"Whoa!" The exhaust blasted as I scooted Samantha's chair off the asphalt and onto the dirt.

"Ladies." He hollered over the engine's rumble.

"Race."

"You hear about Stan?"

"That he is, right now, being miraculously healed for the second time in one glorious summer?"

Race nodded, smiling.

"Yeah, I heard all about it. Doesn't scare me one bit. You?"

"Nah. I figured everything's under control," Race agreed. "I'll pick you up at six if you want to go visit him tonight."

"Let's you and I go spring him out of that place!"

"Whatever you say."

"Get ready to walk right out of that hospital with Stan tonight."

"Okay." Race scratched both dogs' heads and waved at Samantha before gunning it down the road.

We were heading back when the third car came along. What on earth was going on here?

It was a beat-up Cadillac with a couple layers of dust stuck to the paint. It crept up sneaky as a weasel, too, until the last second, when the heat shot clear up the back of my legs.

I whipped around to see a man with shiny dark hair and sunglasses pulling up beside us.

"'Scuse me. I'm looking for a woman named Faith Countryman."

He was a real character. Italian looking, very olive-skinned, with a cigarette between his lips.

"I'm Faith Countryman."

"Hey, hiya. I'm Vico. Vico Cicarrelli." He pinched the cigarette between his teeth when he smiled.

I noticed a tiny old woman then. She sat in the passenger seat, dressed in what looked like black grieving attire.

"My mother, Maria Frances." He nodded toward her.

"Nice to meet you, ma'am."

"Ma here, she don't like speaking English much." Vico looked over his shoulder, then glanced in the rearview mirror. "I'm curious. You heard of me before?"

His mother rolled her eyes and smacked the palm of her hand against her forehead.

"No, I haven't."

"Well, I've been hearing plenty about you."

"Oh?"

He looked around again. "People are saying that you can, well, ya know, *do things*. That you have some kind of special power or something."

"Where'd you hear that?"

"Up at the church."

"The High Hill?"

"Nah. Our Lady of the Sacred Saints . . . the Catholic church." He flicked his ash. "We're heading there right now, matter of fact. Ma here, she goes twice a day. Just in case God hasn't figured out who she is yet."

His mother slapped her knee with disgust, then performed a dramatic sign of the cross.

"She does this gesturing crap all day." Vico waved his hand at her. "But here's the deal. I'm here to inquire about your services for my boss. He says he'll pay you decent, too. Except for Harley Stone up there, he's probably the richest guy in this whole valley. Maybe you heard of him? Giancarlo Galliano?"

This time, his mother clenched her fist and grabbed her upper arm. Then she bit her knuckles, clutching her rosary beads.

"Ma! Stop! You're like a mourning deaf-mute in some wacko signing frenzy!" He turned back to me. "Ma ain't particularly fond of my boss."

"What's his story? This boss of yours."

"Well, you could say he's got a little drug problem. That, and a little hooker problem. With about two tons of paranoia thrown in."

"Where is he right now? Sleeping it off?"

"You could say that too, but with all the coke, the man doesn't really sleep." Vico glanced at the rearview mirror again.

"Sorry, Vico, but I can't help you." I aimed Samantha's wheelchair toward the ranch and began to walk, flanked by a dog on each side.

He tapped the gas just enough to keep up with us. "How much? Name your price. He'd probably give you any amount you asked for."

"Sorry. Not interested."

"What? 'Scuse me, but in your line of work, you gotta be *interested* to help?"

I stopped. "You want a price? Okay, you go tell your boss to give away half his money. Then we'll talk about his problems."

Vico's mouth fell open. "What'd you just say?"

"Half his money. No less. And tell him to show some creativity. He's got a drug problem? Give it to a drug rehab place. He's got a prostitute problem? Fund a shelter for homeless or battered women. Give a prostitute a fresh start, a makeover, a college education. Whatever. Tell him to use his imagination, but to give it away."

"Whoa, Miss Countryman, let's not get hasty or nothin'. There's no way Galliano's gonna go for this."

"That's my price." I began to push Samantha again. "And next time, tell him not to send his flunky to come talk to me."

Vico eyed me over his sunglasses, flabbergasted. "'Scuse me?"

"If this guy's serious, I want to see him in the flesh. I don't deal with errand boys."

"Errand boys?" Vico grimaced.

"Capisce?" I eyed him over my sunglass lenses.

His mother suddenly croaked to life. *"Capisce? Capisce! Parla italiano?"* She kissed her fingertips and flung a big air-smooch at me.

"You speak Italian?" Vico asked.

"Nope," I called over my shoulder. "Only in tongues, baby."

TESTIMONY

VICO CICARRELLI

~

I never cried about my old man leaving us until the summer I met Faith
Countryman. Talk about floodgates. It was as if I was that little kid
again, smelling like macaroni, standing on the curb in high-water jeans,
trying to smile with my lips quivering, and waving goodbye to my pa.

I was seven when he left.

At that age, you're just smart enough to realize that if your pa's cuss-
ing out your ma and going like hell in reverse down the driveway with
his suitcase packed, you're probably not gonna throw a baseball or fish
from a motorboat anytime soon. When Pa ditched Cross Creek, he headed
south and promptly filed for divorce from my ruined-for-the-rest-of-her-life
mother. He wound up in Vegas, working the blackjack tables. Years later,
he mailed me a picture of himself, with his arm around a showgirl. She
was living up to her profession real good, too, cause everything was showing.
And then some.

Ma cried when she saw the photograph, but Ma pretty much cried every day of her life. Sitting at the kitchen table, in full mourning regalia, pounding dough, waving her hands around, and sobbing her eyes out. Those were Ma's most time-consuming activities.

"I cry for everyone," she said in Italian as she wept.

"Ma." I spooned a giant handmade ravioli into my mouth. "Everyone else is trying to enjoy life. Nobody's crying like this."

"Why would they? I'm doing it for all of them." Ma bowed her head in prayer, then popped open an eye. "Especially for you, Vico."

As a teenager, you could say I went looking for a father figure but ended up with Giancarlo Galliano instead. He had a job for me and pockets full of cash, but not exactly the attributes of a saint when it came to being a positive influence.

I was sixteen that first time.

"Vico, all you gotta do is pick up the package in Oakland. Take it to the City. Turn around. Get back home." He patted my cheek with his open palm. "And don't forget to watch your back."

"What's in the box?"

"Never mind."

The sad truth was, Galliano took better care of me than my pa ever did, if that's saying anything worth two cents and a lousy buck.

Ma wasn't exactly first in line to show her appreciation. "Diavolo!" she'd scream at Galliano on Main Street or through the window at the Coffee Pot, while he sat eating elbows and olive oil.

"Ma, the devil? Please."

Galliano had the drug operation, plus hookers, bars, and strip joints in a half a dozen towns, some across the river and a couple over in the Bay Area. He lived in Cross Creek where the cops would never think of looking. Dipping into his merchandise led to full-blown addiction, paranoia, and raging hypochondria, all of which kicked him squarely in the balls on a regular basis. He constantly called his doctor, swallowed strange pills, and even pulled his pants down at three o'clock in the morning for shots in his butt! Yeah, lucky me, being an eyewitness to that sight! Try wiping that vision off your memory bank! Anyway, after a while, the doctor couldn't take it anymore, and he moved his family in the middle of the night to another state.

So, one hot afternoon that summer, we were sitting in our wife beaters and slacks, playing poker in the basement of Our Lady of the Sacred Saints with the priest and some other dedicated parishioners. After the confessions died down and the Communion wine ran out, someone mentioned the new broad in town. Faith Countryman.

"I heard she's the one who got Stan Jackson up and moving, and she did something freaky to that little Parker kid's arm, too."

"I heard she'll stop and pray for you right on the spot."

"I heard she touches you like God Himself."

That was it. Cutting up his coke that night, Galliano couldn't stop with the idea that had suddenly up and crawled inside his head.

"Faith. Countryman. Faith. Countryman." He chanted, all the while snorting more stuff up his nose than I'd ever seen him do—through a rolled-up hundred-dollar bill, too. A couple hours later, he was crying like a one-legged stepchild and promising to quit forever. Right. Like I'd never heard that one before. This time, as if to prove it, he tossed all his blow in the toilet, along with that hundred-dollar bill!

Over the next couple days, his obsession with this Countryman broad escalated to the level of ridiculous.

"Vico, you gotta find her! Get her! I don't care how you do it. Nab her. Seduce her. Marry her. Buy her!" he screamed at me, his eyes bulging like a couple of poached eggs.

"Okay, okay, I'll see what I can do."

That's how I ended up at her side that day, cruising real slow in my Caddy, watching her take a morning walk down River Road. When she finally stepped toward the car to shake my hand, all I could think was that she was pretty spunky for such a class act. Right there, she broke the mold, instantly becoming one of the most interesting broads I'd ever met. And take my word, I'd met my share.

That afternoon, Galliano's bubble was burst to bits when he heard what Faith wanted him to do.

"Half my money? She really said that?" He sat on the couch in his boxers with all the shades drawn, running his fingers through his hair until it balled up like a humongous Brillo pad. "Exactly how did she say it?"

"How many times? Like I told you. She said, 'Tell-him-to-give-half-his-money-away.'"

"Half?"

"Half." I lit a Kool. "Like charity or something. What do I know?"

Galliano sat very still, then took a deep breath. "Tell me again, what was she like?"

"She was something, okay? Like nothing we've ever seen around here."

Slowly, Galliano stood up and put on his pants. "Start the car, Vico."

"We're gonna go get her?"

"Yeah, but first we're going wherever we gotta go to give half my dough away to some pathetic slobs."

∾

After a full day at Stone Ranch, I needed to shake a leg in order to visit Stan Jackson in the hospital one county over. Swooping up my driveway, I found surprise drop-in company waiting in the shade of my front porch. Lucinda Merriweather and Pam Parker had settled deep into the cushions of the wicker furniture. With tongues wagging and faces smug, they acted like they had all night to linger at my front door.

"Well, what brings you two here this evening?" I cut across the grass, past the "For Sale" sign, to the porch.

Lucinda scratched Solomon behind the ears. "Don't mind us, Faith. We're just getting down to the root of something before we tug it on up."

"Trying to solve a couple of mysteries we've stumbled across," Pam added.

Both of them had strange expressions on their faces.

"What's going on?" I asked, stepping up to join them.

Lucinda spoke first. "Well, for starters, that piano playing of yours. I think it's got me, oh, I don't know, energized or something. Since you've moved in, I've whipped up one needlepoint after the next. Never been so productive in all my life. See for yourself." She pressed her hand on top of the stitched cloth she'd displayed on my wicker coffee table.

"I see."

"Now," Lucinda said softly. "Get down there and really look, Faith."

I bent lower. "Very nice, Lucinda."

"Closer." She spread her fingers flat over the piece of work.

I was already close enough to pick the stones out of her ring with my teeth.

"Closer."

"Lucinda, I can't very well see the work with your hand covering it up."

"Well, what do you see then?"

"Your fingers."

"Yes?"

I gasped. "Your incredibly straight and smooth fingers!"

No longer was Lucinda's hand gnarled with swollen, arthritic knuckles. She stretched her fingers straight, then revealed the ornate needlepoint underneath. It was a perfect rendition of the Victorian, woven white against a blue sky, with a gold dog sleeping beside a black door.

"Oh, Lucinda." I held her hands in mine.

From the other wicker settee, Pam cleared her throat.

"You okay, Pam?" I asked.

"Oh, I'm fine. Except for that bone I'm choking on, 'cause I didn't get around to picking it with you yet." She regarded me suspiciously.

"Oh?"

"Now it's my turn to provide a visual." She slipped an X-ray out of a large manila folder. "That right there." She tapped the slick sheet. "That's my boy Ronnie's arm."

I peered into its shadowy image. "Okay."

"No offense, but I've been pretty bugged-out ever since that night we met at the park and Ronnie flew off the monkey bars."

"I see."

"Remember what his arm looked like when he hit the ground? It was sticking out sideways."

I nodded.

"I was fit to be tied, too. Then you came along and a couple of hallelujahs later, Ronnie was okay. In fact, he was great." She studied my face. "Two days after that, he hit two doubles and a single over at Riverdale Park. Brought in four runners. Best game of his life."

"You must be very proud."

"You would think so, wouldn't you? But for the life of me, I couldn't shake the feeling that something was weird about this. So today, I dragged Ronnie into Dr. Halstead's office."

"And?"

"He took one look at this X-ray and asked how on earth Ronnie'd ever broke his arm this bad and fixed it up so good without the family doctor knowing diddly-squat about it."

"Really?"

"Turns out Ronnie's arm was broken, all right. In three places, too. In the very recent past. Halstead confirmed it. And here's the kicker. Supposedly, the doggone thing's magically healed itself. Even on the growth plate, which can be tricky. The only proof it was ever broken are these white lines here." Pam pointed on the X-ray again.

"Hmmm."

"Dr. Halstead said it looked so perfect, the Good Lord must have set those bones Himself."

"Hmmm."

Lucinda spoke up. "So, Pam and I were just wondering if there's something you'd like to tell us."

I glanced at my watch, realizing there was no time for a lengthy explanation.

"Just so you know," Pam added, "Travis didn't even want me coming over here. Said you were probably a witch, or possessed by the Devil."

I dropped into a chair. "Okay, here's the deal . . ." Just then, Race McGee's Chevy thundered up Smith Street and bounced off the curb with a screech.

"Better yet, come see for yourselves!" I pulled them to the car, where, without objection, they climbed right in. Then we held on for dear life as Race gunned it to the hospital one county over. To save Stan Jackson from the valley of the shadow of death. All over again.

～

"Room seven," said the scowling nurse at the front desk.

"Hallelujah," I whispered, deliberately touching her hand with my fingertips. "That's the Lord's number, you know."

She glared, yanking her hand away from me. "Floor two. The elevator's broken. Take the stairs." She glanced at her watch. "Make it quick. Visiting time is over in ten minutes."

The stairs led to the dim, quiet hallway of the second floor, where we tiptoed past the open doors of sick patients.

"Praise the Lord, O my soul . . ." I whispered a psalm as I glanced at an elderly female patient, lying flat on her bed, unconscious, mouth gaped open.

"Lucinda, Pam, start your praising now." I took a deep breath. "Before the miracles come. Throw some faith around this place. Let it lead the way. That's how all this works."

We kept moving down the hall.

"Oh, praise His holy name . . ." I continued the psalm, looking at a little boy in the next room with a medicinal bloat, greenish skin, and eyes like slits.

". . . and forget not all His benefits . . . He forgives all our sins . . . He heals all our diseases . . ."

An old man could barely lift his head to watch us pass.

Room seven was softly lighted above the bed where Stan lay very still. He was breathing through an oxygen mask, hooked up to various monitors and contraptions.

"Oh, now, this is a fine sight!" I shook him awake with a jerk. "Stan, wake up and explain yourself!"

Stan's eyes shot open.

"Get up! We got ten minutes before Nurse Ratched from *The Cuckoo's Nest* comes in here to give us the boot."

Stan tried to sit.

"So, what happened?"

"I guess I got sick again."

"What were you thinking?"

He shrugged.

"No, I mean, like, what *exactly* were you thinking?"

"Well, first, I was thinking how lucky I was to be divinely healed, just like you said. Man, I believed it, too. Then I started feeling awful about my life. How screwed up I've been. All my drinking. How badly I treated my wives. I had three of them, you know? I really didn't deserve to be healed."

"So you condemned yourself. Pronounced yourself guilty. Sentenced yourself back to sin and sickness and death."

Stan sighed as he watched me pour ice water from the pitcher on his tray into a cup.

"Did you forget about this, too?" I dribbled the liquid onto his bald head.

Stan shivered as the water streamed down his face and onto his hospital gown. "Isn't this a cruel thing to do to a guy with complications of pneumonia?"

"Oh, sure, confess pneumonia all over yourself, too. Pneumonia, guilt, death, sins, drinking, Rotten Husband Syndrome. Anything else?"

Stan shut his eyes.

"Listen to me, Stan Jackson." I leaned in close to him. "That night at your place, you were healed. Baptized with the Holy Spirit. To believe anything else is an insult. A slap in the face of our dear Lord. You think He wanted to hang on that cross to endure this same ol' sickness for you not one, but two times? Get real."

I turned my back and started for the door.

"I don't think I can do this anymore, Faith."

"You think you did anything last time?"

Stan stared.

"Don't fool yourself, Stan. You and I? We just went along for the ride."

Pam and Lucinda moved next to Stan and placed their hands on his head.

"Come on, Race. Get over here," Pam prompted.

At the foot of the bed, Race reached with two fingers to grab Stan's big toe poking up under the blanket.

Suddenly, Nurse Ratched was at the doorway, glaring at us. "What do you people think you're doing in here?"

"We're just trying to bless our friend." I touched her shoulder, but she shook me off again.

"Well, this all looks very strange. It's time for you to go, anyway. Visiting hours are over."

"Maybe we could have just a couple more minutes?"

"No. Those are the rules. Time to go."

"It's okay." Stan's voice spoke above the noise of rustling sheets. "Let's get outta here, you guys." Standing beside his empty bed, he had tossed aside his oxygen mask, unhooked his tube connectors, tied the belt of his robe, and scooted into his slippers.

"What the . . . ?" Nurse Ratched protested. But we ignored her and walked out the door and down the hallway. Floor Two suddenly ceased to be as quiet as before.

"The Lord is my Shepherd . . ." Stan's voice sounded strong and clear again.

"Hallelujah." I tried to keep up with him.

"Good luck, Stan," said the old man, now standing at his door.

I squeezed his hand as we passed, and he followed us partway down the hall.

The sick boy came out, too, still swollen and discolored, but slapping Stan a high-five.

The old lady sat up and waved at us from her bed.

"He restoreth my soul." Stan waved back.

Downstairs at the exit, Lucinda suddenly stopped me. "Shouldn't we go back and say something more to that mean old nurse? She could really use some help."

I held the door for her. "Oh, Lucinda, let's face it. Not every wretched sourpuss gets to squeeze his or her butt into Heaven. Lord knows, it'd be a holy mess-pile up there!"

The door slammed against the jamb behind us.

With Stan riding shotgun this time, I climbed in back with the women. Rounding the first curve, we stared at the hospital in the dark. The lighted glass elevator was empty, but it was working now, moving all by itself, floating up from the first floor to the second.

≈

In no time flat, I discovered that Harley Stone had one oddity that caused me to stop and wonder. He was absolutely dead set against answering the telephone. That thing would be ringing off the hook, six, seven, eight times, while Harley fiddled around, doing anything but answering the phone. Meanwhile, I'd be at the kitchen sink, up to my elbows in raw, slimy chicken skin, with salmonella bacteria ready to splatter all over the Stones' kitchen. And once again, I would have to stop, scrub up, and go answer it.

"Harley," I sighed, tripping over the edge of the rug before snatching the phone on the seventh ring. "No offense, but have you had your ears checked lately?" Immediately assaulted by a dial tone, I plopped the receiver back on its cradle.

"Huh? What?" Harley joked, smiling up from his desk.

"The phone. It's blasting like a three-alarm fire bell. I'm starting to wonder if you can hear okay."

Harley leaned back in his chair. "You think maybe I'm missing something by not listening to the voice on the other end?"

"Well, you certainly could be." I laughed. "But we'll never know now. They hung up."

"Guess it wasn't important then." He walked to the warmer for a handful of biscuits, then headed for the back door. He turned to smile at me. "The way I figure it, everything I need, I got right here. Everyone I care about is under this roof. Al handles all my business calls at his office. So whatever some jabbermouth wants to tell me on the phone can wait." He waved a biscuit and stepped off the porch. "See ya later, Faith."

"Hey, Harley, how 'bout I jot down a message if anyone calls on that telephone of yours?"

"Would ya?" He shot me a grin.

Married or not, it was impossible not to notice how easily his smile widened.

With that image threatening to linger around in my head, I figured the best way to sidetrack my thoughts was to hang out with Harley's family members for a while. First, Samantha and I sat in the living room at the window, where together we watched the creek roll by. Then I small-talked with Kyle, inside, outside, and one room to the next before he finally settled in front of the TV. What really did the trick, though, was leaping headfirst into one of the most despised household chores ever concocted by some harebrained chambermaid from days of yore. Closet cleaning. Deep, dirty, and utterly distracting.

Hours later, when enough junk and holey jeans had tumbled down on my head, I was ready for a break. Hauling the bags to the bins out by the barn, I spotted Harley across the creek. He was steering a tractor through the olive groves, shaking weeds loose with the rake on the back. He whipped off his hat, to wipe his forehead and the back of his neck.

Feeling sorry for him in the heat of midday, I crossed the bridge with a glass of lemonade on ice.

When Harley checked the rake trailing behind him, he saw me, stopped the engine, and climbed down from the tractor. "What's up?"

I handed him the lemonade. "Figured you might be thirsty."

Harley looked both surprised and grateful. "Thanks." He swigged. "Everything okay in there?" He glanced at the house.

"Kyle's over at Ronnie Parker's house. Samantha's resting. Dinner's in the crock. And two of your four walk-in closets are now officially purged and cleaned." I took a deep breath of the late afternoon air. "You need any help out here?"

"Oh, sure," Harley quipped. "How 'bout you hop up there and handle the next couple rows while I drink my lemonade under that tree?"

"Okay." Within seconds, I'd already climbed into the tractor seat and twisted the starter key.

"Whoa, hey, I'm kidding."

"I'm not. Sit there and take a break. I know how to do this."

He shook his head. "No, it's too dusty out here."

I laughed. "You've got way more dust in those closets of yours, believe me."

"Wait." Harley set his glass on a stump. "I can't let you hang yourself on an olive branch, or something." He threw his leg up and landed behind me in the seat.

"Ready?"

"Let's go."

The engine grumbled back to life. Harley offered brief instructions on tractor maneuvering through an olive orchard on a slight grade. I strained to hear him over the hum of the motor, while aiming straight down the middle of the path.

At the edge of the row, he plunked his ranch hat on my head, and slid down. "There. Now you really look like you know what you're doing."

"Okay, let's see if I've got this." I adjusted the brim, pushed the gas, and aimed between the rows while Harley sat on the stump, shaking his head every time I passed.

Three rows later, I stopped the rig. Harley helped me to the ground. "Nice job, Faith."

"I used to drive my daddy's tractor all the time when I was a kid."

"In Modesto?"

I was shocked. "You know where I'm from?"

"You kidding? Newcomers are dissected worse than lab frogs around here. Gossiped about from the Mill to the Monkey Bar and everywhere between."

"No way."

"Yep." He cocked his head, chuckling. "I bet I can give you an earful about the mysterious woman who moved to Smith Street in Cross Creek this summer."

"All right, let's hear what you've got."

"You are Faith Countryman. Some distant relative of David Doone. He died and left you everything."

"No relation whatsoever. I met him down south, and he gave me the Victorian on Smith Street."

Harley's eyebrow arched. "Must have made quite an impression to inherit a house worth a quarter million bucks."

"A hundred and fifty grand, if my real estate lady knows what she's doing."

"You put the place up for sale the minute you got here."

"It was several days later, but yeah."

"Cross Creek is a temporary home for you."

"Just for the summer."

"Your best friend is that guy over there." Harley smiled at Solomon, who'd followed me across the bridge. "You play a mean piano. You've lived in Hollywood."

"Santa Monica, actually."

He looked at my eyes. "You're single."

"Yes."

"That's it. That's what everyone thinks they know about you."

"Good." I smiled up at him. "That's enough. I'd like to hang on to some small shred of that mystery."

"Oh, there was one more thing." Harley climbed up the tractor to grab the key, then jumped down beside me. "Something about praying over sick people?"

"All over them."

"Do they get well?"

"Most of the time. Some folks, though, they're just itching to be miserable, whether they know it or not."

"You're not like one of those people we see on television, are you?"

"Exactly like them. Right now, I'm gonna go spray up my hair in a massive updo and glue on some false eyelashes."

Harley laughed. "So, you just pray and hope for the best?"

"Well, there's a little more to it than that." I squinted at the sunset slashed orange behind him. "I guess you could say, I have a strong belief. I'm willing to stick my neck out, to make a fool of myself even, in order to get someone released from an infirmity. I'm available to provide faith for those who don't have enough, or any at all. When it comes to getting your prayers answered, it's crucial that there's someone with some faith nearby."

The olive trees shuffled their leaves in the breeze.

"I don't think I've prayed in years," Harley murmured. "Not since Samantha's accident." He drained the rest of his lemonade.

"That's a long time."

"So, is that why you're here?" he suddenly asked. "To pray for Samantha?"

"I don't know. It's hard to tell what's going on when you're in the thick of things." I paused. "It's not the only reason I'm here, though."

"Oh?" His eyes widened.

"'Cause, besides those closets packed to the gills, and all that other stuff waiting inside that big ol' house of yours, I'm gonna have to pray for your ears to open so you'll start hearing that telephone when it rings."

He laughed as I tossed his hat to him, and we started back to the house.

"Hey, Faith."

"Yeah?"

"If you want to pray for Samantha, go right ahead. She needs all the help she can get."

There on the curve of the bridge, with the night coming on lush and silver, the torrential heartache of his situation hit me. I couldn't help but feel for both of them. For Samantha, so terminally damaged. For Harley, suffering beside her.

"Of course I will, Harley. Matter of fact, I'm already on it."

~

That evening, while I snoozed on my sofa, someone came banging like crazy on the front door.

"What?" I leaped to my feet.

Solomon growled, scrambling to the door beside me.

Oh no.

Through the peephole, I saw Vico Cicarrelli. He was smoking a cigarette and running his fingers through his dark wavy hair.

I flung open the door. "Did you do it?"

"Do what?" He flashed me a smile.

I slammed the door in his face.

The knocking sounded again.

Jerking open the door a second time, I was pushed aside by Solomon, who stepped over the threshold with a fit of wild barking.

"So?" I waited for Vico's answer.

"'Scuse me?" Vico squinted. He exhaled a hazy plume off the porch. "Uh, okay, I'm just here to continue our little chat about you helping my boss, Mr. Galliano, with his, you know, medical ailments."

Parked at the curb was Vico's drab-looking Cadillac. Inside, I saw his mother's worried-sick face at the passenger window. Some guy sat in the back seat, peering at us with wary eyes and a big ratty bird's nest of a hairdo.

"Vico, I'm kind of tired tonight, so just answer me this. Did you do it?"

"By 'it,' are you talking about Mr. Galliano giving away half his money?"

"Bingo."

"Well, funny you should mention that, because since we last talked, I've actually researched biblical giving according to the Good Book. And I gotta tell ya, insisting we unload half of Galliano's money is a pretty extravagant request."

"Oh really?"

"Why stop there, ya know? How 'bout we throw in a couple pints of blood or donate an organ while we're at it?"

I slammed the door, faster and harder this time.

Vico knocked while shouting through the closed door. "Ten percent is the usual tithe."

Throwing the door wide, I took one step, plucked the cigarette from between his lips, and flipped it into Solomon's water bowl.

"You think you're so smart, huh, Vico? Well, you go back to the Good Book and look up the part about how it's easier to squeeze a camel through the eye of a needle than it is for a rich man to gain entry into Heaven. Then when you've delivered half of this man's money to various needy causes, you come and talk to me about his sicknesses, addictions, afflictions, hang-ups, hangnails, and whatever else he's got wrong with him." I tried to shut the door.

"Wait." Vico stuck his arm in the door jamb. "Let me get this straight." He glanced back at the car. "You're refusing to see Mr. Galliano until he gives away exactly half of his money?"

"That's right. Same thing I told you last time. And keep quiet about it. Don't brag and tell everybody. That kind of giving doesn't really count." I watched him stand there bug-eyed, combing his fingers through his hair again. "How close to half are you two meatballs right now?"

"Us two meatballs? We're at ten percent. You know, like the tithe," he retorted sarcastically.

"Well, then," I said as I patted his shoulder. "You're off to a great start."

Vico shook his head, then slowly broke into a smile. "Tell me something, Faith Countryman." He pulled a fresh cigarette from his pack and edged backward down the steps. "Are you really a faith healer? Or just a ball buster?"

"You'll just have to wait and see." I tugged Solomon's collar gently. "Till then, keep giving that money away." I waved at his mother, who erupted with a huge smile, then threw me a kiss, and folded her hands in prayer, bowing her head.

"Vico," I yelled after him. "You guys just keep giving till it hurts."

"Yeah, yeah." He swung open the driver's door.

"A bunch of money's no different from a big bag of seed," I hollered. "You gotta scatter it around or it's worthless, baby."

～

It was the morning after our tractor ride. I greeted Harley in the kitchen, put on a pot of coffee, threw the first pile of clothes in the washer, rubbed spices on a pot roast, and began to tidy up the family room where Samantha stared at the television from her wheelchair.

"Morning, Samantha." I knelt to adjust her more comfortably in the seat.

Other than that, she didn't move.

No doubt about it, Samantha was a spooky little fraction of the dark, stunning woman she'd once been. Skin and bones, silently blinking like a Halloween skeleton. As I set her feet into position, I studied the massive scars and discoloration that streaked across her knees and calves.

"Samantha, you poor thing." I patted her hand. "How on earth did something so horrific happen to you, anyway?" I walked away, leaving her alone with the neatly coifed news anchor who bellowed the morning headlines.

Harley was waiting for me in the kitchen. "One sweeping act of infidelity. That's how," he softly said.

"What?"

"That's how something so horrific happened to her."

I dead-stopped in the middle of the room, staring, trying to comprehend what he was saying.

"Samantha had an affair. Well, actually, she probably had a few. This particular time, it took place at a couple of thousand feet." Harley leaned against the counter. "I wouldn't recommend it to anyone, especially when the pilot's participating."

"No wonder they crashed."

"Yeah, no kidding. His name was Ryder Manning. He died on impact. He was some rich guy from Lake Tahoe, with planes and boats and a mansion on the North Shore. Samantha grew up there, too, just as privileged and spoiled as he was."

"Really?"

"She and I met skiing at the top of Heavenly. We got married within a few months. Way too soon. We didn't know what we were really doing, I guess. She hated ranch life. Being stuck out here alone. She was always gone. Traveling, shopping, socializing at the lake. Then Kyle was born, and a few weeks later, she got reacquainted with Ryder Manning."

"What on earth was she doing with this guy?"

"Besides trying to liven up a scenic flight over the lake? Who knows? Samantha was beautiful then. Real charming. Very controlling, though. She always had to be the center of attention, the object of everyone's desire."

"How sad."

"Life is strange, isn't it, Faith?"

I looked up at him. "Yes, it is."

"You're going along, dumb enough to think it's gonna be one way forever. Then out of the blue, things go sideways. Planes crash. The world changes. Just when you least expect it."

Harley's high cheekbones and strong jaw set firm. His eyes darkened. He seemed to be looking straight through me. Or past me, as if seeing something else. But I saw it, too, something deeply familiar reflecting. Split seconds. Bad choices. Wrong people. Regrets. Shame.

"And then nothing is ever the same." He shook his head.

Except for all that shame. I know. Until healing comes.

I waited for him to continue.

"After the accident, Samantha's mother tried to have her attorneys dissolve our marriage. She wanted to take Samantha back home to the lake, hire a staff of nurses, or maybe even put her in a convalescent home. She never dreamt I'd handle everything myself."

"She offered you an out?"

"Yeah, but there was a big hitch to it. She wanted Kyle, too."

"No way."

"I'm not sure if she wanted full custody, or what. I didn't let her go on about it. Told her no flat out, and told myself I would do whatever it took to keep my son here with me, even if it meant keeping Samantha as my wife."

"You've done a great job. Kyle is wonderful."

"I love that kid." Harley stared out the window. "He's what I live for."

At lunchtime, the light washed warm yellows across the Stones' nook as Harley and Kyle sat across from each other at the table. With legs stretched out, they chewed their sandwiches, while slowly, strategically moving checkers across a black-and-red board.

"You guys look like a couple of bookends hunched over that game." I poured a glass of iced tea and began to clean up the kitchen.

Kyle's light-blond bangs flopped over his eyes when he looked up. "Bookends?"

"Maybe not identical bookends." I smiled. "But a nice complementary pair."

"Ronnie Parker's dad has bookends made out of real ram horns," Kyle told his dad.

"Wow." Harley scrutinized his next move. "Be careful reading over at their house. You're liable to be gored!"

Kyle smiled across the board.

"You've been spending a lot of time at the Parkers'." Harley waited for his next turn. "You and Ronnie are pretty good friends now, huh?"

"Yeah. He's cool."

"Good."

"And I like Pam, too. She's nice. She does all kinds of mom stuff for us."

"Mom stuff?" Harley asked. "What kind of stuff?"

"Well, like, all the stuff that you and Faith do for me here, I guess. Except she sits and talks to us about everything."

"Everything?"

"Yeah, like about our lives and how we feel about things." Kyle jumped Harley's black checker. "She makes us really think."

I watched as Harley studied his son, nodding.

"Sometimes, I just wish I had a mom who could ask me how I'm doing or how I feel about something, ya know?"

"Yeah, I know, Kyle."

With the conversation swerving into serious territory, I started for the door.

"Where are you going, Faith?"

I turned around. "I'll be back to bake cookies in a bit. I'm just going to go finish cleaning the rest of those closets."

"Don't run into any skeletons," Harley called after me.

Kyle's frowned. "Skeletons?"

"Skeletons in the closet." Harley laughed. "Just a figure of speech."

~

I found the skeleton on the highest shelf in the guest-bedroom closet. Covered with dust, it was buried in a deep box labeled "Photographs & Albums." Call me a big fat snoop, but after all the broken toys, deflated balls, holiday decorations, and abandoned clothes, taking a few minutes to look at someone else's photos seemed pretty harmless.

Harley and Samantha's wedding album captured a glimmering day next to an icy blue Lake Tahoe. The bride defined ravishing, giggling under a mist of rice. Harley looked like a magazine model with his tuxedo tie loosened, leaning against a redwood deck. Another album revealed Kyle, red-faced and towheaded, on the day of his birth. Then a shot of the three of them at the Stone Ranch gate at River Road. Samantha was standing up in the picture. She was poised and holding her son in her arms. Doing simple things she would never be able to do again.

One item remained in the bottom of the box. I wiped Samantha's journal with the dust rag. No matter how down and dirty and possibly criminal it was to read someone else's diary, it was far too tempting to ignore. So off I went, into the previous mindset of the younger, healthier Samantha Stone.

Early entries included, "Harley is wonderful, but why, oh why, do we have to live out here in the sticks? I'm so homesick for the lake and all the parties. Cross Creek is dullsville!"

For a moment, I imagined Samantha realizing the difficult shock of a small town like Cross Creek.

Then it was, "I'm pregnant! Harley is thrilled beyond belief! Me? Not so much."

Samantha was "wild about" her "handsome Harley" but "sick to death of chores" and "painfully bored on the ranch"—or "out here in the pit of Nowheresville," as she called it. She looked forward to "going lakeside" after Kyle's delivery, and to "shopping like a fiend again" in San Francisco.

"Mother bought a new Mercedes sedan for the baby and me!" she wrote. "Harley says the ranch is too dusty for fancy cars, but I've got to have *some* fun, don't I?"

Despite her wealth, beauty, and high-society upbringing, Samantha sounded so empty and sad.

Then came the date of Kyle's birth, written in bold capital letters with exclamation points, and Kyle's tiny wristband from the hospital nursery attached with tape. Descriptions followed, with details of Kyle's first few months of life.

I turned the page. Out fell a photograph of a man who gazed up at me from the floor. "Hmmm," I whispered. "And who might you be?"

I already knew.

The man was so blond, you could practically see through his hair, with white eyebrows against his tanned complexion. He wore a leather aviator-style bomber jacket and a smirk for a smile. And without a doubt, except for the age difference, he was the spitting image of now ten-year-old Kyle Stone.

~

Later, when the Stones' closets could've passed a military inspection, I completely switched gears. Going into the kitchen, I began to beat the absolute daylights out of a cube of softened butter in the bottom of a mixing bowl. I couldn't erase the sneering face of the man in that picture from my mind. Ryder Manning. The man Harley had told me about. The pilot who'd had an affair with Samantha, then crashed his plane with her and died on impact. The man who looked more like Kyle Stone than Kyle Stone did.

I pummeled the butter with the wooden spoon. It was all so obvious now. Harley, with his dark looks, the brown hair, olive skin, and mahogany eyes. Samantha, with even darker features, her black hair, midnight blue eyes, and thick lashes. Then out comes Kyle with a rosy complexion, a crop of white hair, sky-blue eyes, and almost invisible lashes and brows. The boy was a dead ringer for his dad—not the man who'd loved and cared for him all of his life, but the man who was, no doubt, his biological father. Ryder Manning.

With Kyle blaring the TV volume in the next room, I began furiously whipping all of the cookie ingredients. Slowly, the flour moistened with the wet mixture. I wiped a stream of tears on my arm, smacked the batter to smithereens, then wiped my eyes again. The whole thing was so incredibly sickening. Here was Harley, wonderful and decent, yet unattainable to any other woman. Shackled for life to a woman who'd not only betrayed him, but must have tricked him into thinking he was the father of their son. It was despicable!

"You got something against that cookie dough?" Harley asked suddenly from behind me.

I spun around, completely rattled from my thoughts.

He smiled and held out a glass of lemonade. "Thought I'd return the favor from yesterday."

I took the glass and finished it in one single drink.

"You okay?"

"I'm fine. Thanks a lot, Harley."

When all was said and done, hot dang, if it was not the best batch of cookies I'd ever baked. With each scoop of the spatula and slide from the hot sheet to the cooling rack, I couldn't stop thinking of Harley, and Samantha, and Kyle. I ended up thinking about them long after I drove home. Away from the sweet smell of the Stones' kitchen, where cookies laced with sugar and lumped with chocolate sat waiting for a family whose husband and father was desperately trying to hold things together.

$$\sim$$

Prayer wasn't made for sissies.

Mama used to say so all the time, and to prove it, she'd point out the members of our most mature and tightly linked prayer chain at the First Baptist Church. "You see those little hunched-over blue hairs over there? Don't let 'em fool ya. They'll unleash more tangible power than you can shake a stick at. Using nothing but the forces of faith and patience, those old birds can sit on their duffs and bring wayward husbands and teenagers home, report card grades and bank balances up, and all field crops to harvest right on time."

Morning after morning I was back into full-tilt prayer posture on the floor. Food-fasting, forgiving anyone I ever knew, petitioning from the core of my being. Ancient foreign tongues moved out my lips, lifting the people of Cross Creek. All of them. The Stones. Samantha. I couldn't think of a woman who needed prayers as much as she did. Samantha was a burdened soul, about as guilty as they come, caught red-handed, instantaneously punished and crippled for life, only to be reminded of her sins and crimes every minute of every day. For some reason, knowing all this made me love her more.

Solomon's toenails clicked on the floor beside me. I heard him sigh, as if he, too, was grasping the reality.

That things were different now. More sad and serious than before.

~

Attendance was skyrocketing at the Church on the High Hill. All because of Stan Jackson, who before the summer wouldn't have been caught dead in church, not counting his three misguided wedding ceremonies, all of which culminated in crash-and-burn divorce proceedings. In the time since he'd unhooked the gadgets, ripped out the tubes, and walked out of the hospital one county over, he'd made a full and miraculous recovery, one that displayed glorious evidence of a spiritual healing in the natural realm. But hold on to your hat, because word on the street was that Stan had benefited otherwise. In some freakish late-life vertical growth spurt, he'd managed to stretch an entire two-inches and one-eighth in actual measurable height. Amen to that, because his raging Napoleon complex couldn't have helped with those wifely problems. To top things off, Stan's hair was coming back brown and wavy, like he was twenty-five again and ready to take on the world.

With Stan walking around a changed man, it didn't take long before the folks in Cross Creek were knocking on their noggins, trying to figure out what was going on. So Pastor Alexander Mosley, not being a man to miss an opportunity for evangelistic advancement, invited Stan to give his personal testimony of salvation and healing at the podium in front of the entire congregation at the Church on the High Hill.

At first, members were skeptical. "Whoa! Wait a minute. Who?"

"You mean, Stan-my-best-friend-is-Jose-Cuervo Jackson?"

"We'll need more faith than the size of a mustard seed to believe this one."

Stan's conversion and continuing physical transformation was exactly the sort of news that traveled fast, especially when Race McGee was zipping down Main Street telling anybody who could hear over the reverberations of his souped-up Chevy. Lucinda Merriweather shot right out of the beautification chair at Dot's Beauty Spot, her head full of pin curls, to get the details since his hospital stay. From that point, the news took on a life of its own. Traveling its course, moving shop to shop, down one aisle and up the next at the Mill, and even into the dark, smoky interior of the Monkey Bar, just as Pam Parker was swallowing a glass of Bud Light with her husband, Travis.

She later told me that she fessed up right then and there. "I was part of this, Trav. I was with them. At the hospital that night. I touched Stan with my own hands." Travis just stared, lingering in her eyes, then kissed her cheek, and motioned the bartender for another round.

By Sunday morning, there were more people at the Church on the High Hill than Christmas Eve, Easter Morning, and baby dedication Sunday combined. Right on time, too, because ever since Stan Jackson's miraculous transformation, Pastor Mosley had plucked straight out of his thinking cap a big, brilliant, brand-new idea.

"Brothers and sisters." Mosley's voice boomed into the microphone atop the altar stairs. "We at the Church on the High Hill have an announcement. There's going to be an old-fashioned tent revival! Right here, in just a few weeks!" He pounded the podium with his fist. "Get ready to have your socks blown off!"

With that said, a tomb of dead silence ensued. Like everyone's stomachs had suddenly seized up on them. Then coughs and squirms tore across the sanctuary in a ripple effect. An old-fashioned revival sounded like two tons and a truckload of old-fashioned work. Throw in a big tent, and you're bound to pile on headaches galore.

Much to my surprise, in the middle of all that empty quiet, it was me who popped out with what could have easily been classified as the spiritual gift of encouragement. "Hallelujah!" I heard myself say just as loud as could be from the back row.

Applause rang up to follow.

As Mosley went on to further explain his plan, people began to lean forward, to listen, and to nod their heads. Something warm and heavy spilled into the place. The Spirit. The Holy Ghost. Sparking interest, flaming excitement, moving like angelic wildfire.

"Where have all the old tent revivals gone, anyway?" a clearly rejuvenated Pastor Mosley questioned, throwing his hands into the air.

"Amen," a voice up front agreed.

Then more applause.

"Those tents were places of profound signs and wonders. People practically got saved and healed right out from under themselves, behind their own backs. It was that powerful, that contagious."

"Glory be!" someone in the crowd shouted.

"Even today, in third world countries, people are often healed instantaneously, simply because of their anticipation to get to a tent preacher. They'll walk for days to the tent to receive their miracles. Sometimes, they're healed halfway there because of the spirit of expectation." Mosley stared solemnly at the group before him. "That, my friends, is what we call faith."

Mama's voice sounded its familiar verse in my head. *Faith. The evidence of things unseen.*

"Amen."

"Say it, Pastor. Preach it."

"And speaking of healing miracles, Cross Creek has its own real live miracle walking in our midst this summer."

The side door next to the choir risers suddenly flew open. Out strutted a slightly taller, nicely filled out, brown-haired, very vibrant-looking Stan Jackson.

My very own spirit of expectation must have been previously askew, because my mouth fell down around my kneecaps just like everyone else's. A miraculous transformation of the first degree stood before us at the podium. Stan hardly resembled the bald little man who'd recited the Twenty-Third Psalm from his deathbed, or the one who walked out of a hospital one county over.

A slight commotion stirred behind me. Harley Stone had just come through the door, with Kyle right behind him, pushing Samantha's chair. They quietly parked her in the center aisle as I scooted over to make room for them.

Harley gave me a quick smile before putting his full attention on Stan.

"I've got a confession for you," Stan said confidently into the microphone. "I thought the next time I was dragged to church, it'd be in my own coffin."

Polite laughter hummed through the pews.

Stan paused, then lowered his voice. "Imagine your biggest idea of a second chance. Imagine life, if only it could have worked out for you. Life, the way you might have hoped it could have been."

I breathed the soapy smell of Harley next to me. I wanted to whisper to him something about Mosley having too much caffeine this morning, or that Stan was turning out to be a rather amazing public speaker. But all I could think of was the photograph I'd found in the closet of the man who was a dead ringer for Harley's son. I sat up straighter in my seat.

Stan clutched the podium with both hands. "Earlier this summer, I was filled up with cancerous tumors. Now I've been given the most amazing second chance. My doctors can no longer find proof of any cancer or tumors. Not in the tests, or the scans, or in any medical exams. And now I'm filled with something else."

"Amen."

"Until lately, I never thought about God. I didn't pray or read the Bible or ever even think about that kind of stuff."

"I hear you, brother!"

"Then someone new to Cross Creek forced me to change. Her name is Faith Countryman, and I believe she's here today. Faith?" Stan squinted into the audience. "Come on up here."

Harley slanted an eyebrow my direction.

I started down the center aisle as Mrs. Marble played "Go Tell It on the Mountain" on the organ.

Stan and I bear-hugged while Mosley said, "Ladies and gentlemen, Faith Countryman will be the one praying for all the sick people at our Revival's healing meeting in a few weeks!"

What? Wait a minute!

Huge applause interrupted my thoughts.

I noticed Lucinda Merriweather then, fanning herself near the front. And Pam Parker, who waved and whispered to her husband, pointing at me.

"Faith Countryman has a powerful gift, and she'll be using it mightily as she heads up what could be the most moving night of the Revival! Of our whole summer perhaps!"

Hold on! What?

Other introductions quickly followed, including the rest of those Mosley had obviously bamboozled into leading or organizing various components of the upcoming Revival Weekend.

At last, he brought his family up there. Mrs. Mosley, a mousy little woman who cringed at the attention. Their teenaged daughter, Mindy, who was dressed in black, with spiked hair and so many piercings, it looked like she'd just tripped in Bob's Bait Shop and landed on a fully stocked tackle box.

One glance, and I couldn't help but reach for her hand.

"Brothers and sisters, mark your calendars. The Revival on the High Hill is scheduled for the last weekend of August. I'm asking every single one of you to help in order to pull it off. But glory be, the hardest part's already been squared away. A couple of generous souls have offered to foot the entire bill. Two Cross Creek residents, who insisted they remain anonymous, said they were looking high and low for a charitable cause to give *half* their money to. You heard me! Half! Now, how's that for faith in action?"

The sanctuary exploded in the loudest cheers yet.

I saw them. A couple rows back was the man I had a hunch was Giancarlo Galliano. Next to him, Vico Cicarrelli sat eyeballing me, his poochy lips grinning. Vico's mama patted his shoulder, then clenched her praying hands till her knuckles went white.

"Nobody's off the hook here, folks," Mosley continued. "We need every last one of you to volunteer. Babysitters, baptizers, and barbecuers. Cooks. Musicians. Drivers. Sunday school teachers. Carpenters. Tent raisers. The sign-up sheet is outside. Don't you dare leave this place today without putting your name on it."

Mrs. Marble played the chords for the benediction.

"By the way, the whole world's invited to come!" Mosley was beside himself with excitement. "Now what we really need is some good old-fashioned press coverage!"

TESTIMONY

HUGH SPANO

~

*A*ll I wanted to do was survive this assignment and get out of town. I tried ignoring the fact that it was the most beautiful morning I could remember in a long time. Turning onto Smith Street, I found an avenue checkered with manicured lawns, gingerbread houses, and clean driveways. Some anal-retentive freak of a paperboy had delivered newspapers dead-center on every porch. It looked like a scene straight out of the good life, as if no one there would ever have a worry in the world.

"Oh yeah?" I muttered. "Just wait."

I was an expert on the things that could sneak up and kill you. I'd made my living off of them. Inked their startling headlines across newspapers. Aired their gory details on TV newscasts. These things were terrifying. And they were everywhere.

I wiped my sweaty palms on my walking shorts. The walking shorts I'd never walked anywhere in, unless you counted the distance from my couch, to the refrigerator, to the can.

Parking my car under the shade of a tree, I climbed out and sighed. This time, I couldn't blow it. Not if I ever wanted big breakers, hot features, First Columns, and impressive bylines again. Not if I wanted my dignity back. Besides, there was a really cool light that ricocheted off everything in this weird little town. This street, in particular, really sparkled with it. I adjusted my lens and snapped at least a dozen pictures, zooming in on big porches with screen doors. On flags flying red, white, and blue. On kids who smiled in the morning sunshine. Real artsy stuff. Not that I'd ever have any use for it.

The temperature was cranking up fast, but so far, I hadn't succumbed to heat stroke. My initial boredom with Cross Creek two days prior was replaced by mild curiosity. Now, for some strange reason, I found myself in a surprisingly decent mood. And I hadn't even taken my meds yet.

I slung my bag over my shoulder and rang her doorbell, stiffening as a dog barked, and again when I heard her shoes on the other side of the door. I waited. For the handle to turn. For us to get this over with.

My intent was to do Faith Countryman "quick and dirty." In news jargon, that meant get the story and get out. Fast. Move on to the next issue, accident, catastrophe. Go. But on this day, the door opened, and I was as flabbergasted as anyone that my plans could alter. That in a split second my assignment would, entirely on its own, demand a fresh perspective and begin to rewrite itself.

That's what the best stories always did, of course. Wrote themselves. I'd never forget my first, when I was just a kid. The one about Dee Dee, the lady down the street, who gave me shivers when she smiled and then died trying too hard.

"Hughie, we're all just like Dee Dee, searching in our own ways," Mother said on the day the coroner rolled Dee Dee up in a sheet like a burrito, slid her into his van like an oven, and drove away with her forever.

Dee Dee.

"Short for Delilah," she'd informed my mother over cocktails one summer afternoon on our back patio. "Like the lady in the Bible who

seduced Samson, made him cut his hair and lose all his powers of massive strength." She winked at me through Pall Mall smoke, as if the demolition of a man's powers with one haircut was something to boast about. I watched her sip her drink, realizing that Dee Dee had done similar things right on our block. Stripped the strength and control out of all the men. Who could resist a woman with lips outlined in pink like a Valentine heart? With her long, graceful legs, tanned smooth and brown? Her panting husband bought her a new car every time the wind blew. The paperboy climbed off his bike every day to make his delivery face-to-face. Even my dad loaned her his pointy-blade shovel, and he never let anyone borrow garage stuff.

"Dee Dee was always trying something new, Hughie," Mother explained at the kitchen counter the day they laid her to rest. "A new religion. A new wardrobe. She constantly changed her style, her opinion, her hairdo. A few husbands. All those cars. Doctors. Shrinks. Psychics. You name it, and she went around the world looking for it." Mother slammed the oven door on a beige funeral casserole. "Overdose . . . well, I guess that was something new, too."

Mother's lips were void of any pink and as tight as a piece of elastic. "Someday you'll find yourself searching for something too, Hughie." She pointed her oven mitt at my face. "Just make sure it doesn't kill ya, okay?"

It was then that my own search began. I typed up "Dee Dee's Death" for my seventh-grade English essay and received an A+ and stellar compliments from the teacher, including, "I like the way you think, Hugh Spano."

At first, I went hunting for another Dee Dee, for anyone who could liven things up. But as it turned out, I was looking for a story. A perfect story. But such stories didn't really exist. Until Cross Creek, and the summer of revival when this unusual woman opened her front door and sucker punched me with her joy.

Imagine my shock. After years in a business that dropped my jaw to my collar on a daily basis. News was one of the biggest highs a person could *legally get, and I was no different from anyone else in the business. I'd come for the stories, but I'd stuck around for the constant kick. The worse the state of affairs, the hotter the news day. The more disgusting the topic, the more provocative the tease. The closer to deadline, the more tangy the jab of adrenaline. All day long, the blood charged madly through our veins, while off we ran on complete overload with too much information, pounding the door down, trying to make the final cut.*

"It isn't brain surgery!" the news director would scream above the clatter of television monitors, news wires, typewriter keys, and police scanners. "Just make it happen! And hurry up!"

Random events of the day controlled everything. They dictated whether we built real news stories out of piddly garbage, or cut substantial pieces to bare bones. In television, I stretched stories about nothing to in-depth, three-and-a-half minute, reporter-tracked packages with fancy graphics and stand-up wraparounds. Later, at the Sun, *I made short bits of insipid squat stretch down the page and end up like poetry.*

Deadlines crept closer. The news junkies went crazier. Slamming typewriters. Throwing things. Screaming and hollering. At the Sun, *a pregnant woman broke her water minutes before her column was due, but even that didn't stop her. No one else batted an eyelash either. They just glanced at the clock and stepped around her puddle. We'd all seen worse. We'd researched, read, written, and photographed worse. There wasn't one of us who hadn't trudged through heartache, dead bodies, and six feet of turds for the sake of a story. That was the very nature of our business.*

Okay, so it wasn't brain surgery. But I knew better. I was well aware of the fact that the simple task of relaying information to a media-sucking public could kill a guy from the inside out, one current event at a time.

Years ago, if you had tried telling me that some lady out in the middle of the sticks, who smelled like fresh peaches, would direct my intrigue back to the core of a simple human-interest story, well, I'd have laughed in your face. But who knows? Because I wasn't exactly laughing much back then.

I'd tell you this, though. When Faith Countryman opened the door that morning and took my hand in both of hers, it was more than just a polite greeting between two strangers. She had me. She held me. And I held on right back. For dear life. For every story I had ever loved and for those that had nearly killed me. Suddenly, in the middle of that heat, I was shivering again, as if Dee Dee were back, winking, smoking, sipping a cool drink, stripping the power right out of me.

When I finally let go, we walked across the countryside for hours. Slowly, my strength returned, and the only story that would ever really matter fell right into my lap and began to materialize.

~

Almost as soon as Pastor Mosley had requested press coverage for the Revival, I had a big-time city-slicker reporter named Hugh Spano knocking on my door, looking like he'd rather have been anywhere else.

I led the way down Smith Street. "Are you a walker, Mr. Spano?" We headed toward the river and the foothills as our interview session got underway.

"A walker? No. But I might need one by the time we're finished here today." He gave me a wry smile and strode beside me, notepad in hand, camera cases slapping against his waist and thigh.

Hugh Spano was a good sport. Solomon proved that first thing, knocking the poor man on the grass and licking his face clean.

"You don't walk over there in San Francisco, huh?"

"Does up a flight of stairs to my apartment count?" Hugh breathed heavily, trying to keep up.

Solomon trotted alongside us as we started up the grade.

"So, Faith, why don't you tell me about this big old-fashioned tent revival coming up at the Church on the High Hill."

"Well, this really is Pastor Mosley's deal. I'm just helping out with the healing service on Saturday night."

"And this so-called healing ability of yours? You honestly think it's some legitimate thing?"

"Oh, heck yeah. But first of all, it's not my ability. God is the one who does the healing. I'm just there to provide intercessory prayer, support, and encouragement. My only ability might be that I believe so much. That's the faith part. Sometimes that's all God's looking for. Someone who's willing to take Him at His Word."

"Why do you do this?

"Well, it's right there in the Bible. We're supposed to pray for the sick."

"Wait, stop here, Faith." Hugh adjusted his focus and clicked off a few shots. "Boy, the light is so unusual in this place. It absolutely sparkles." He stared through the viewfinder. "It's actually bouncing right down on you."

I laughed, and smiled straight into the camera. "Are you a believer, Mr. Spano?"

Snap.

Hugh wiped his brow with the back of his hand. "No, you'd have to call me a skeptic. I prefer facts."

I studied Hugh's face as he concentrated on the light, angling for his next shot. Then it dawned on me. "There's something very familiar about you, Mr. Spano."

"I was on air in San Francisco a long time ago." Hugh sighed when he saw the next uphill grade. "The California affiliates used to pick up my pieces. Maybe you saw them."

"How'd you get into this line of work?"

"I was a news writer. Going on air was a fluke. I happened to be the only sober guy in the newsroom wearing a necktie the day the mayor's son was kidnapped for ransom and finally released. Our regular anchor was on his office floor sleeping off a martini lunch. I went on camera for ten hours straight that day."

"Exciting, huh?" I gestured for Hugh to cut through a thicket of trees to the riverbank.

"Yeah. That anchor ended up in rehab, and I got the gig. I really immersed myself in those stories. It was always emotional for me."

Hugh fiddled with the buttons on his camera, catching me off guard with a candid shot.

"Nice," he said. "My editor will love these. We don't get a lot of glamorous people way back yonder on the Religion page."

I smiled, pointing, keeping him moving along the edge of the river toward hillier ground. "What took you from TV to the paper?"

"My career took a turn." Hugh frowned.

"I see."

"There was just so much bad news. Too many murders to count, let alone report. The homeless were freezing to death on the wharf. AIDS was killing off entire neighborhoods. Gangs were waging wars. Kids had guns, drugs, and babies. Earthquakes, plane crashes, and nukes. *E. coli*, mad cow, flesh-eating bacteria."

We stopped on the bridge. The water below skimmed the rocks. Solomon sat down next to Hugh's shoes, head tilted up, blinking at him.

"Then one Christmas," he said as he scratched Solomon's ears, "a 95-year-old nun was beaten to death on the street. No one bothered to help." He shook his head. "Same day, a cop friend of mine was shot in a drive-by, waiting in line for a cup of coffee." His voice cracked. "Then that night, there was this family." He spoke slowly, deliberately. "On public assistance. Their scraggly little Christmas tree caught fire, destroying everything in their apartment. The presents those parents saved all year to buy. Everything." Hugh paused. "Both kids were killed." He lowered his head. "I can still see those flames."

"Oh," I breathed out.

Hugh's voice quivered. "I couldn't take it anymore. Not one more story. I snapped. Came completely unhinged. Barricaded myself in an edit bay with a loaded shotgun, put the video on a continuous loop, locked the door, stripped down to my jockey shorts, and started to cry. I didn't move for three days."

I gently touched Hugh's shoulder as he stared over the edge of the bridge.

"The whole thing turned into a police standoff, and I became the subject of one of our news stories. My own friends and coworkers covered it nonstop."

We stood for several minutes. Until Solomon rubbed his head against Hugh's knee and the wind began to stir.

Ever so softly, I broke the silence. "So, you're telling me I'm alone in the woods with a complete nutcase right now?"

Hugh's eyes popped wide open.

We took one look at each other, and began to laugh. Exploding laughter from a deep reserve. Tremendous belly laughs. The kind that hurt so bad, you could pull a muscle or snap blood vessels in your cheeks. Finally, we tried to compose ourselves, holding our aching stomachs, wiping our noses and eyes.

"Faith Countryman, I have not laughed like that in as long as I can remember."

"Neither have I. I'm so glad I met you, Hugh. What a wonderful day you've given me."

"You too." Still laughing, he wiped the dust off his lens. "You're going to make one fantastic story."

I took his hand and pulled him back up toward the path. "Hugh Spano, are you still thinking you came here for a story?"

Snapping his camera case shut, he eyed me.

"We're gonna make a believer out of you before you leave this place. And you can quote me on that, baby."

∽

An article about a future church event wasn't exactly hot-off-the-press breaking news, so the *San Francisco Sun* was in no rush to go to print